A. L. O. E.

Idols in the Heart

A Tale

A. L. O. E.

Idols in the Heart
A Tale

ISBN/EAN: 9783337030650

Printed in Europe, USA, Canada, Australia, Japan

Cover: Foto ©Andreas Hilbeck / pixelio.de

More available books at **www.hansebooks.com**

THE SICK-CHAMBER.

IDOLS
IN THE HEART.

A Tale.

BY

A. L. O. E.,

AUTHOR OF "THE GIANT-KILLER," "PRIDE AND HIS PRISONERS,"
ETC. ETC.

"Keep yourselves from Idols."—*1 John* v. 21.
"Covetousness, which is idolatry."—*Col.* iii. 5.
"Set your affection on things above, not on things
on the earth."—*Col.* iii. 2.

London:
T. NELSON AND SONS, PATERNOSTER ROW.
EDINBURGH; AND NEW YORK.

1883.

Contents.

————o————

IDOLS IN THE HEART.

CHAPTER I.

THE ARRIVAL.

"MY dear girls, I can indeed enter into your feelings," said Lady Selina Mountjoy in a tone of sympathy; "it is trying to have to welcome a stranger to your home, to see her take the place once occupied by your dear departed mother."

"It is not so much that," interrupted Arabella with some abruptness, "but—"

"I understand—I understand perfectly," said Lady Selina, with an expressive movement of the head; "if your dear papa had chosen differently—some one whom you knew, valued, could confide in —some one, in short, of your mother's position in life, to whom you could look up as to a second parent, it would have been very different; but the orphan of a country doctor—so young, so inexperienced—to have her placed at the head of an establishment like this, is—   But I ought not to speak thus; of course your dear papa has chosen very well, very wisely; no doubt Mrs. Effingham is a very charming creature;" and the lady leaned back on her cushioned chair, folded her hands, and looked into the fire with an air of melancholy meditation.

Vincent, the youngest of the party, a boy about eleven years of age, had been sitting at the table with a book before him, but had never turned over a leaf, drinking in eagerly every word uttered by his aunt on the subject of the step-mother whose arrival with her husband was now hourly expected in Belgrave Square.   He was a bright, intelligent boy, in whose blue eyes every passing emotion was mirrored as in a glass, whether the feeling were good or evil.   The expression of those eyes was neither kind nor gentle as he said abruptly, "Didn't you tell us that her grandmother was a French-woman?   I do hate and detest everything French!"

"Her own name—Clemence—is French," observed Louisa, the younger of the two girls who sat, with embroidery in their hands, before the fire, with their feet resting on the bright fender for the sake of warmth, as the month was November, and the weather cold.

"Yes," sighed Lady Selina, "it is true. Her grandmother was a French refugee,—of course a Papist; and, no doubt, her descendant is tinctured with Romish errors. No fault of hers, poor thing!"

"She's not a Roman Catholic," said Vincent quickly. "Don't you remember that papa said that she was a great friend of the clergyman at Stoneby, and helped him in the schools and with the poor? He would not have let a Papist do that."

"My dear child," replied Lady Selina, languidly stirring the fire, "I never for a moment imagined that your papa would marry one who was avowedly a Papist; but, depend upon it, there will be a leaning, a dangerous leaning. We shall require to be on our guard, there is such a natural tendency in the human heart towards idolatry. As to her having helped Mr. Gray, that was very natural— very natural indeed. She was glad to make friends, and the clergyman and his wife were probably her only neighbours. Besides, in a dull country place there is such a lack of occupation, that young ladies take to district visiting to save themselves from dying of ennui."

"Oh!" exclaimed Louisa, "after such a dismal life, what a change it will be to her to come to

London! How she will delight in all its amusements! I hope that she'll be as mad after the opera
as I am; and that from week's end to week's end
we may never have the penance of an evening at
home, except when we entertain company ourselves!
I can forgive anything in her but being dull, sober,
and solemn."

"Giddy child!" lisped Lady Selina, with uplifted
finger and affected smile, "you sadly need some one
to keep you in order—some one to hold the rein
with a firmer hand than your poor indulgent aunt
ever has done."

"Hold the rein!" repeated Arabella with indignant pride, the blood mounting to her forehead as
she spoke. "I hope that Mrs. Effingham will make
no attempt of that kind with us. There's but five
years' difference between her age and mine; and as
regards knowledge of the world, I suppose that the
difference lies all the other way. I have no idea of
being governed by an apothecary's daughter!"

"Nor I!" exclaimed Louisa, shaking her pretty
ringlets with a contemptuous toss of the head.

"Nor I!" echoed Vincent, shutting his book, and
joining his sisters by the fire.

"Little rebels!—fy! fy!" said their aunt, with
a smile on her lips that contradicted her words.
Lady Selina saw that she had succeeded in her aim.

She had prejudiced the minds of her sister's children against the young bride of their father; she had created a party against Clemence in the home which she was about to enter as its mistress. Arabella, Louisa, and their brother, would be on the watch to find out defects in the character, manners, and education of their step-mother; they would regard her rather in the light of a usurper, from whom any assertion of power would be an encroachment on their rights, than as a friend united to them by a close and tender tie.

It was not, perhaps, surprising that Lady Selina should contemplate with little satisfaction a marriage which dethroned her from the position in Mr. Effingham's house which she had held for seven years. Lady Selina had enjoyed more of the luxuries of life and the pleasures of society in the dwelling of her brother-in-law, than her small capital of ten thousand pounds could have secured for her anywhere else. To Vincent Effingham it had been a satisfaction to have at the head of his household a lady of position and intelligence, who would take a general superintendence of the education of his three motherless children. How far Lady Selina was fitted to do justice to the charge, is a different question. She was one who passed well in the world when viewed only in its candle-light glare—one to whom had been applied the various epithets of "a sensible woman," "an amiable creature," and "a very desirable acquaintance."

Lady Selina had acquired the reputation for *sense*, from those whose opinions resembled her own, for her tact in steering clear of every theological difficulty. Her religion, if religion it could be called, was of the simplest and most easy description. To her the path to heaven was so wide that its boundaries were scarcely visible. There was, of course, a decent attendance to forms, for that the laws of society demanded; nay more, Lady Selina had about half-a-dozen cut and dried religious phrases, to be brought forward before clergymen and serious visitors, and put back again immediately upon their departure: these were, perhaps, satisfactory evidence to herself that her condition, as regards spiritual things, was one of the most perfect security. Enthusiasm on any subject regarding a future state appeared to the "woman of sense" a weak and childish folly. She could understand a politician's strong interest in his party, a landlord's in his estate, a lady's in raising her position by a single step in the social circle; but the longing of an immortal soul for peace, pardon, and purity, was a matter completely foreign to her experience, and beyond her comprehension. Lady Selina wore her religion as she did her mantle; it was becoming, fashionable, and commodious, and it could be laid aside at a moment's notice if it occasioned the slightest inconvenience.

And Lady Selina was called "an amiable creature" by such as are easily won by a polished manner and courteous address. She possessed the art of being censorious without appearing so. She seldom openly expressed an unfavourable opinion of any one; but conveyed more sarcastic meaning in a word of faint praise or disparaging pity, a shake of the head, a hesitating tone, or a soft, compassionating sigh, than might have been expressed by severe vituperation. None of her strokes were direct strokes—she never appeared to take aim; but her balls ever glanced off at some delicate angle, and effected her object without visible effort of her own. She had a secret pride in her power of influencing others, never considering that her ingenuity simply consisted in the art of gratifying malice at the expense of generosity and candour.

Lady Selina was "a very desirable acquaintance" to those who only knew her as an acquaintance. Her kindliness was as the blue tint on the distant mountain, which vanishes as we approach nearer towards the barren height. Whoever might rest upon her friendship, would lean, indeed, upon a broken reed. But, in the exchange of ordinary courtesies, in the art of simulating cordiality and sympathy, Lady Selina was a perfect adept. Few left her presence without a feeling of self-satisfaction and gratified vanity, which caused both the visit and her to whom it had been made to be remembered with pleasure.

The woman of the world's ideas of education were the reflection and counterpart of her views on religion. To her, the first object in life was to shine in the world ; and, accordingly, so far as young people were trained to accomplish this object, so far she deemed their education complete. Arabella and Louisa were provided with a French governess, and the first masters in music and drawing ; and their aunt, with the air of one who feels that she has conscientiously performed an arduous duty, spoke to her acquaintance of her anxious and indefatigable efforts to do full justice to her motherless charge. It is true, that occasionally a moral maxim or religious precept dropped from the lips of Lady Selina for the benefit of her sister's children; such was the caution against the heart's tendency to idolatry uttered in the preceding conversation. The words had been lightly spoken, and their meaning weighed neither by speaker nor listeners ; but whether they might not with advantage have been applied to the consciences of all, will be seen in the following narrative.

The marriage of Mr. Effingham with Clemence Fairburne, a young lady whom he had met in Cornwall while on a visit to a clerical friend, was to Lady Selina an unwelcome event. Notwithstanding, however, the complaint that she rather insinuated than expressed to her numerous acquaintance, that her wealthy brother-in-law had united himself to one possessing neither fortune nor high position, it is probable that Lady Selina would have been far more annoyed had his second wife been equal in rank to his first. Clemence was young and unacquainted with the world. She would probably enter into society with the diffidence of one to whom its usages were not familiar. Lady Selina, like some astute politician of old, foresaw an extension of her own regency under the minority of the rightful sovereign. She determined that Clemence should be a mere cipher in her own house, and follow instead of leading ; she should occupy as low a position as possible in the eyes of those over whom circumstances had placed her. Artfully and successfully Lady Selina impressed the family, and even the household, with the idea that Clemence was some low-born, half-educated girl, whom Mr. Effingham had had the weakness to marry, because she possessed a few personal attractions ! On the few hints thrown out by Lady Selina others enlarged—they filled up her lightly sketched outlines. The French governess, Mademoiselle Lafleur, shrugged her shoulders in the school-room, ventured to breathe the word *més-alliance* even in the presence of her pupils, and directed the flow of her conversation perpetually on the theme of the miseries inflicted by tyrannical step-mothers. Arabella and Louisa began almost to look upon themselves in the light of injured parties, because their father, still in the vigour of life, had sought to add to his domestic happiness! Their prejudices would have been still more strong and bitter but for the young wife's letters, which reached them from time to time, and which breathed such a kindly spirit, such a desire to know and to love the children of her dear husband, that even Lady Selina's insinuations could scarcely destroy their effect.

And now the day appointed for the first meeting of Clemence with her new family had arrived ; every-thing in the house was made ready for the reception of the master and the lady of his choice. There was the bustle of preparation in the lower regions of the dwelling ; the harsh voice of Mrs. Ventner, the housekeeper, was pitched to a sharper key than usual ; while in the drawing-room a restless sen-sation of expectation prevailed, which prevented Lady Selina and her nieces from settling to any of their usual occupations. The piano had been opened, but its keys were untouched; the needle pressed the embroidery, but not a single additional leaf gave sign of progress in the work.

The short November day was darkening into twilight; the yellow lights round the Square started one by one into view, faintly gleaming through the cold white haze. A few snow-flakes fell noiselessly upon the pavement, along which, at long intervals, a foot-passenger hurried, wrapping his cloak tightly around him to fence out the piercing north wind. Vincent took his station at the window to give earliest notice of the arrival, while Lady Selina and his sisters chatted around the blazing fire.

"Here they are at last!" exclaimed Vincent, as a chariot dashed up to the door, with dusty imperial and travel-soiled wheels, and horses from whose heated sides the steam rose into the chill evening air. "Here they are!" he repeated, and swinging himself down the stairs, he was at the hall door almost before the powdered footmen who were there in waiting had had time to open it. The ladies more slowly followed; but curiosity with Louisa getting the better of dignity, she ran lightly down the long broad flight of steps, and found Vincent returning the affectionate embrace of her who longed to find in him indeed a son.

CHAPTER II.

HAT were the sensations of the fair young bride when she crossed the threshold of that lordly dwelling, when she entered the spacious and luxurious apartments which she was thenceforth to call her own? Clemence looked round her with admiration on the many beautiful things which adorned her husband's home. She who from childhood had known little of luxury, saw, with the fresh pleasure of girlhood, inlaid tables spread with elegant specimens of the arts of many lands—mosaics from Italy, porcelain from Sevres, the delicate ivory carving of China. The exquisite paintings on the panelled wall, the grand piano with the graceful harp beside it, even the luxurious furniture, the crimson drapery of the satin curtains, and the rich softness of the velvet carpet, impressed Clemence's mind with an idea of beauty and grandeur to which a girl not quite one and twenty years of age could scarcely be insensible. Frankly and artlessly the bride expressed her admiration, knowing that to do so would gratify her husband, who listened with a pleased smile ; and yet her warm young heart was conscious of some feeling of oppression, some sensation almost resembling that of fear ! The coldness with which her two step-daughters had received, not returned her kindly kiss,—the frigid courtesy of Lady Selina, —had had much the same effect upon Mrs. Effingham's spirit as the cold November mist upon nature. Clemence could not feel at her ease, though the natural grace of her manner prevented her shyness from betraying her into awkwardness. She could not but deem it a relief when at length she could retire to her own apartment ; and dismissing the maid, who pressed forward with officious offers of assistance, Clemence seated herself upon a sofa, and endeavoured to collect her scattered thoughts.

"I wish that they had been younger !" was almost the first idea which took definite shape in her mind ; "little ones who would have nestled into my heart, and who would have won and returned all my love ! I am afraid—but how foolish, how wrong it is to let a shadow of anxiety or fear dim the brightness of a day which should be one of the happiest of my life ! We shall love one another;

yes, we must—we shall!   *His* children cannot but
be dear to me, and I will earnestly try to gain their
affections; and if I am weak and inexperienced, and
utterly unequal to perform rightly the duties of this
new, strange state of life, is not my heavenly Father
as near me here as when I was in the dear old
cottage?"   Then, sinking on her knees, with clasped
hands Clemence returned fervent thanks for the
boundless blessings which Providence had lavished
upon her, and implored for wisdom and aid, and for
favour in the sight of those with whom she was now
so nearly connected.

Clemence rose from her devotions joyous and
hopeful, and proceeded at once to do that which she
regarded rather as a pleasure than as a duty.   Un-
locking her little travelling-case, she took out writing
materials, and hastily penned a note to her uncle,
Captain Thistlewood, the guardian of her orphaned
youth, announcing her arrival at her home.   Clemence knew how impatiently the letter would be
watched for, and how eagerly welcomed by the old
sailor; and as she placed within the envelope an
enclosure, addressed to the care of her former pastor,
she smiled to think how many hearths she would
warm, how many boards she would spread in Stoneby, and how many a family would bless her in the
village where she counted as many friends as there

were poor. "Oh! this is the luxury of being rich!" thought Clemence; and carrying the letter in her hand, with a light step and light heart she descended the staircase. The joy which she felt in sending her remittance was purer and brighter than any which merely personal gratification could have bestowed.

"She's no more French than I am!" muttered Vincent to himself, as he gazed on her fair brow and clear blue eyes. His prejudices were fast melting away beneath the spell of that sunny smile.

The sound of the gong now summoned the family to a sumptuous repast. Notwithstanding her disposition to be pleased with everything, Clemence, at the head of the table loaded with plate and glittering with crystal, felt her timid misgiving return. It was not so much that the young wife found the unaccustomed presence of powdered servants oppressive, that her new state was irksome to her, and that it seemed as if freedom were exchanged for grandeur; but that, with intuitive perception, she had become aware that her every word and movement were watched and criticized, and that by no friendly eyes. Mr. Effingham was a silent man—that evening he was more silent than usual; Arabella and Louisa sat as if unable to open their lips; the chief burden of the conversation fell upon the young timid woman, whose heart fluttered with the·excite-

ment of her new position, and her anxiety to say
nothing and do nothing that could possibly shock or
offend.   Lady Selina, indeed, repeatedly broke the
silence which, notwithstanding the efforts of Clemence, frequently fell on the circle; but, whether by
design or not, she so directed the conversation as to
puzzle and embarrass the bride.

"I think that the estates of the Marquis of Bard-
ston lie near Stoneby."

"Very near to the village," replied Clemence.

"Does the picture of the old marchioness by Sir
Joshua Reynolds deserve its fame?" inquired Lady
Selina.   "I have often wished to see it; of course,
you have very frequently done so!"

"I was never in the Castle," answered Clemence;
"it is not opened to the public."

There was something disagreeable to the bride,
though she scarcely knew why, in the slight bend
of the head and pursing of the lip with which Lady
Selina received her straightforward reply.   The lady
of fashion seemed determined to discourse that evening upon no subject but that of the various connections of persons of rank.   Her memory appeared unusually at fault.   She could not remember whom
Lord Greenallen's sister had married, or what had
been the family name of the Duchess of Dinorben,
and was ever referring for information to poor Cle-

mence, who had never looked into a peerage in her life. Mrs. Effingham felt herself painfully ignorant of everything that Lady Selina seemed to think it quite necessary to know, and was heartily glad when, the tedious ceremony of dinner being ended, the party adjourned to the drawing-room.

Vincent was the only one of her new acquaintance with whom Clemence was quite at ease, and she was heartily sorry to find that he was to return to his school early on the morrow, having only come home in order to be introduced to his step-mother. She could rest her hand on his shoulder, and her kind and playful words would call up an answering smile on the face of the boy; but his sisters' monosyllabic replies to her questions, the marked manner in which they always addressed her as "Mrs. Effingham," chilled and discouraged the young wife, while she felt an increasing mistrust and almost dread of their polite and dignified aunt. There was, likewise, something repellent to the frank and open nature of Clemence in the flowery compliments, the exaggerated politeness, with which Mademoiselle Lafleur, who joined the circle at tea, received her courteous greeting. Clemence secretly reproached herself for foolish prejudice, but could not shake off a sensation of repulsion. Weary with her journey and the excitement of the meeting, Clemence rejoiced when the

long evening closed. She was startled at the sound
of her own sigh, as she sat listlessly before her toilet-
table; and unconsciously raising her eyes to her
mirror, saw reflected there her own pale face, marked
with a thoughtful and anxious expression.

"What a child I must be!" exclaimed Clemence
half aloud, "to let such trifles weigh upon me—I
who have everything to enjoy, everything to be
thankful for!" and she struggled, and not unsuccess-
fully, to throw from her spirit its burden, and to look
upon the untried future before her with cheerful
confidence and hope. Had Clemence fully on that
evening realized the difficulties of her position, her
heart would indeed have sunk within her. A youthful servant of the Lord, she stood alone in a house
where faith in Him had hitherto been nothing but a
name; she had entered a family where every heart
had a secret idol set up in its inmost shrine. Clemence looked up to her husband as to one all wisdom
and goodness. Mr. Effingham bore in the world a
spotless name; he was liberal in his charities, and
appeared earnest in his profession of religion. His
young wife, with loving, trusting confidence, had
twined her heart's affections around him, as some fair
creeper clasps with its tendrils a stately forest tree.
No suspicion crossed her mind that any unworthy
passion could have place in a heart that she deemed

the abode of every virtue—-that the tree so goodly to the eye could nourish a destroyer within. With different eyes would Clemence have surveyed all the expensive luxuries of the banker's mansion had she known— But we must not anticipate. Clemence was not the first woman, nor will be the last, whose affections have blinded her judgment, whose fond credulity has invested the object of her choice with the noblest and highest qualities of man. Alas! when the cold touch of experience awakens the loving spirit from such a blissful delusion!

CHAPTER III.

FIRST STEPS.

"OH, Arabella!—mademoiselle!" exclaimed Louisa on the following day, as she entered the school-room at a later hour than usual, "I have been so much diverted—I have been enjoying such a rare treat!" and she threw herself into an arm-chair, and gave way to a burst of merriment.

"Qu'est-ce que c'est?" inquired the governess.

"I have seen Mrs. Effingham's trousseau!" cried Louisa. Arabella looked up from her drawing, and the exclamation of mademoiselle expressed her curiosity on a subject which is supposed to be one of some interest to the fair sex.

" I was passing the door of her dressing-room," continued Louisa, "and as it happened to be ajar she saw me, and called to me to come in."

"As one school-girl might another," said Arabella contemptuously.

"And there was the bride on her knees, herself unpacking her boxes!"

"She has not been accustomed to many servants," observed Arabella, "and finds it most convenient to wait upon herself."

"And the trousseau de madame was magnifique, no doubt?" said mademoiselle, with a little irony in her tone.

"Beautiful simplicity!" laughed Louisa; "I suppose that Mrs. Effingham has met somewhere with the line, 'Beauty when unadorned adorned the most,' and has adopted it for her motto!"

"Perhaps," suggested mademoiselle, "the *marchande de modes* at Stoneby—"

"Lived in the time of King Pharamond," interrupted Louisa; "or the bride played *marchande de modes* herself; or, what is more probable still, employed her school-girls to run up her dresses, and make them true charity pattern! There's not a flounce or a fringe in the whole set, from the white silk wedding-dress to the neat cotton-print."

"Cotton-print! est-il possible!" exclaimed mademoiselle, lifting up her hands.

"And the dressing-case—oh!" cried Louisa, bursting into fresh laughter at the recollection.

"Quelque chose très-bizarre—very extraordinary!"

"Ordinary, certainly, without the extra! Brushes, combs, all enclosed in a simple *bag*, ingeniously made, with many pockets big and little, quite a curiosity of art;—I believe it was one of her wedding presents!"

Arabella and mademoiselle joined in the mirth which this idea inspired.

"I should like to have seen *les cadeaux*," observed the latter.

"I saw everything—all her treasures," cried Louisa; "I have a correct inventory of them in my head. The diamond ring which Mrs. Effingham wears is papa's gift; so is the bracelet, and his miniature surrounded with brilliants."

"Oh! but her own family—her own friends, what did they give?" asked mademoiselle.

"Her own family seems to consist of her old uncle, Captain Thistlewood, who presented her with —let me see! an old-fashioned locket containing her parents' hair. It does not look like gold; I think that he must have picked it up at a pawn-broker's. Oh! and she has some distant lady relations, who seem to enjoy a monopoly of making markers—red, pink, and blue; and that she may have no lack of books to put them into, the clergy-man, Mr. Gray, has given her a Church-Service; and his wife—such a present for a bridal! it would have been much more appropriate for a funeral—Baxter's 'Saint's Everlasting Rest'!"

"Anything else?" inquired Arabella with a sneer.

"The gem of the collection is to come. You should have seen Mrs. Effingham unfolding it, and the look with which she surveyed it! A huge patchwork table-cover all the colours of the rainbow. 'My dear school-girls' present,' said she, as tenderly as if each ugly patch had been a love-token set in jewels!"

"I hope that she's not going to display it in our drawing-room," exclaimed Arabella.

"I think that madame should wear it as a shawl —bring in a new *mode*," said Lafleur.

"I wish that I'd thought of recommending that!" exclaimed Louisa, clapping her hands; "she looks so unsophisticated and ready to believe. I'd lay anything that were we to tell her that the hoods of opera-cloaks are worn expressly as pockets to hold bits of bread for distribution to beggars, that such is the approved method of being charitable in London, she would say, with one of her gentle smiles, 'What an admirable plan!' and adopt the fashion directly. I thought of passing something of the kind upon her, but somehow I could not command my countenance when she looked at me with her inquiring blue eyes!"

"I suspect she's sharper than you think," said Arabella shortly.

"Well, she is going to the milliner and dressmaker to-day—she saw the necessity for that; and I'm going in the carriage with her, and Aunt Selina also, I fancy."

"I wonder what pleasure you can find!"

"Oh! it will be the rarest fun in the world! She is such a shy, timid creature, I can see at a glance that she has an awe for my aunt, and is afraid of the sound of her own voice when the earl's daughter is present; so what between Lady Selina, and chattering little Madame La Voye, we'll get Mrs. Effingham into such a whirlpool of fashion, we'll bewilder her so with our *nouveautes*, that she will order anything and everything that we please, and come out into the world so gay that she will not know herself when she looks in her glass!"

The visits to the fashionable dressmaker and milliner were accomplished that afternoon under the auspices of Lady Selina, who, in according her undesired presence, contrived to make Clemence very sensibly feel that she was performing an act of condescension. If Clemence was ignorant of the intricacies of the peerage, she was also entirely at fault in the mysteries of *la mode;* she scarcely knew *moire antique* and *point d'Alençon* even by

name, and the jargon of French terms which flowed
so glibly from the tongue of Madame La Voye,
would have been scarcely more unintelligible to
Mrs. Effingham if uttered in the Japanese language.
This and that rich article of attire, to be adorned in
some incomprehensible style, was recommended as
absolutely indispensable, and in a manner which
left the shy young wife scarcely the option of re-
fusal. If knowledge be power, ignorance is weakness; and Clemence, dazzled, confused, painfully
anxious to please, and shrinking from exposing
herself to ridicule, suffered her own taste and inclination to be overborne by those of her fashionable
companions.

Clemence returned home with the disagreeable
conviction that she had been led into extravagance
to an extent which she was unable to calculate;
for in the presence of Lady Selina she had not
ventured to ask the cost of anything. She felt that
she had yielded with the helplessness of a child to
an influence which her judgment told her was not
an influence for good.

"How exceedingly weakly I have acted to-day!"
such was the mortifying reflection of Clemence as
soon as she had leisure for thought. "I fear that
I have abused the generosity and confidence of my
dear husband, and spent more in selfish indulgence

in one hour than should have sufficed me for a year
True, my situation in life has been changed, and
some things were really necessary; but I was
carried away like a feather on the breeze, afraid to
say what I liked or disliked, afraid to show that I
thought money of any value except as a means of
gratifying caprice.   What a strange, new existence
this is!   I seem to be breathing quite a different
atmosphere—to have entered a world where ideas of
right and wrong, important and trivial, are utterly
unlike those to which I have been accustomed from
my childhood.   Except my beloved husband, there
is no one here to whom I could speak the feelings
of my heart, believing that they would be even
understood.   I wonder if, as I become experienced in
the ways of the world, I shall gradually become like
those around me—if I shall ever resemble Lady
Selina!"   A smile passed across Clemence's face as
the idea first suggested itself to her mind; but it
almost instantly faded away, and was succeeded by
an expression of serious thought.   "I fear that I
am very unfit to meet the temptations of this new
scene.   The world appears to me like a petrifying
stream.   Some spirits, like my noble Vincent's, can
drink of it uninjured, and then rise above it on the
strong wings of reason and faith; but I fear that I
shall be like some weak spray, gradually losing all

inward life, and growing harder and colder as the waters flow by it! These two days have shown me more of weakness and folly, yes, and vanity too, in my own heart, than I was ever sensible of before. I have felt as much ashamed of my ignorance of that which I have never had an opportunity of knowing, as if I had been charged with a serious fault. I have been tempted to equivocation, and have more than once assented with my lips, or by my silence, to that which in my heart I denied. I have felt my vanity gratified even by the silly flattery of one who probably considers flattery as a part of her trade. If I am thus on first entering these scenes, fresh from the instructions of my pious friends, full of the earnest resolutions made before God in my home, what shall I be when time may have weakened the remembrance of those in-structions, the strength of those resolutions? If I stumble at the very first step, how shall I walk steadily and faithfully along a path which I foresee will for me be full of snares? O my God, help me, for I am a weak, infirm child! Let me not forget Thy warning, *Love not the world, neither the things that are in the world.* The difficulties which beset me must make me more earnest in prayer, more diligent in self-examination, more watchful over my deceitful heart!"

Clemence slowly paced her apartment, and wingèd thought carried her back to her childhood's home. "How true are the words which I once heard,—Every new change in the course of our lives, like a bend in a river, brings before us new difficulties, new duties, and new dangers, and shows us our own characters in a new light! I have hitherto been gently gliding with the tide ; and if the banks sometimes appeared a little flat and dull, there was nothing in outward circumstances to shut out from me the light of Heaven. In seeking to please God, I best pleased the dear ones who regarded me with such partial affection. My duties accorded with my inclinations. But now,—my duties, what are they ?" Clemence paused for some minutes and reflected. "I must learn to be able to say 'No'—a painful task, from which my cowardice shrinks ; I must be content sometimes *not* to please, and yet in indifferent matters be as careful—even more careful than ever—not to give offence or cause displeasure. I must exercise the grave duties of a housewife, nor from indolence or timidity shift upon others the responsibilities which God made mine when I became a wife. Mine own Vincent !"—her eye rested on the miniature of her husband—" would that I were more qualified to make his home what that home ought to be ! But

MRS. EFFINGHAM.

Page 32.

he will cheer and encourage me in the attempt to do so; he will have indulgence on my ignorance; he will be my support, my guide, my example; and he will teach me to become more worthy to be his wife!"

CHAPTER IV.

See how the orient dew,
  Shed from the bosom of the morn
Into the blowing roses,
Yet careless of its mansion new,
  For the clear region where 'twas born,
Round in itself encloses;
And in its little globe's extent
Frames as it can its native element.
How it the purple flower does slight,
   Scarce touching where it lies,
   But gazing back upon the skies,
Shines with a mournful light.
   Like its own tear;
Because so long divided from the sphere!
Restless it rolls, and insecure,
Trembling lest it grow impure!

So the soul—that drop, that ray
Of the clear fountain of eternal day—
Could it within the *human flower* be seen,
   Remembering still its former height,
Shuns the sweet leaves and blossoms green,
   And recollecting its own light,
Does in its pure and circling thoughts express
The greater heaven in a heaven less.

In how coy a figure wound,
    Every way it turns away;
So the world excluding round,
    Yet receiving in the day,—
Dark beneath, but bright above,—
Here disdaining, there in love:
    How loose and easy hence to go!
How girt and ready to ascend!—·
    Moving but on a point below,
In all about does upward bend.

OW quaintly, yet how exquisitely, in these lines has the old poet Marvell portrayed those who, *in the world*, are yet *not of the world!* How few, alas! can read their own description in that of the pure bright dew-drop! How many, instead of resting even on the flower, "loose and easy hence to go," waiting till the warm sun "exhales it back again," have dropped from leaf to leaf, lower and lower, till, sinking at length to earth, and mingling with its dust, they are lost for evermore!

About a week after her arrival in Belgrave Square we will glance again at Clemence Effingham. She is in her husband's quiet study—her favourite retreat. The ruddy fire-light falls cheerfully on the shelves of the well-filled book-case, which occupies almost an entire side of the small but comfortable apartment. Cheerfully glances that light on the expansive brow and handsome features of Mr. Effingham, cheerfully on the locks of shaded gold of her who sits at his feet. Clemence, still girlish in manner, and glad to throw off for a brief space the wearisome formality of etiquette, has seated herself on a low footstool, and, resting her clasped hands on her husband's knee, is looking up into his face with a look of earnest inquiry.

"You see, my Vincent, that all is so new to me, —I am so fearful of making mistakes, so conscious of my own inexperience. You must guide and assist me, dearest. Ever since you told me what large sums—to me they seem startling sums—are constantly passing through Mrs. Ventuer's hands, I cannot help imagining that there must be strange waste in some quarter."

"There always is waste in a large establishment; there is no necessity that we should mark the expenditure of every shilling, or enter into the details of every domestic arrangement."

"But supposing that there should be something even worse than waste," asked Clemence in a tone of hesitation, "ought we to place temptations in the way of those who serve us, by exercising no watchfulness over them, by placing such unbounded confidence in them as may be, as is sometimes, abused?"

"Well, my love," replied Mr. Effingham, "exercise

as vigorous a superintendence as you will; keep the machinery in as perfect order as you like."

"It is no question of liking with me," cried Clemence, laughing a little, but not merrily; "for bills and books—tradesmen's books, I mean—I have a horror; and, like Macbeth, I have to screw up my courage to the sticking-point before I venture on a colloquy with Mrs. Ventner. I never had a taste for governing, and the power intrusted to me is almost too heavy a weight for these poor little hands to grasp. I really need the support of my liege lord's stronger arm! I am like a minister of state who has to manage a troublesome House of Commons, and," she added, with a little hesitation, "rather a refractory House of Lords, and who cannot command a majority in either!" Clemence spoke gaily and lightly, but painful truth lay beneath the jest.

"Refractory House of Lords! I see—I see!" said Mr. Effingham, with a smile; "Louisa is a giddy child, and Arabella has a temper of her own. But all will come right—all will come right, with a little patience and firmness. I have the utmost confidence in your sense and judgment, my love."

"I wish that others had," replied Clemence, speaking at first playfully, but her voice becoming earnest and almost agitated as she proceeded. "It is doubtless my own fault, Vincent, or perhaps the fault of

my youth, but it seems to me that my wishes and
opinions are of very little weight in this house.   I
want to consult you on so many points, that I may
know whether I am right or wrong.   Do you think
it well that Louisa should be so constantly out,
especially in the society of those from whom it seems
to me, as far as I can judge, that she can only learn
worldliness and levity?   Her studies are perpetually
interrupted at an age when steady application is
most valuable; and exposure to the night air really
injures her health,—she could hardly sleep last night
on account of her cough."

"Forbid her, then, to go out again till she has
lost it."

"O Vincent, I shall be a dreadfully unpopular
premier!" exclaimed Clemence.   Then she added,
drawing her husband's hand within her own, "If
you, dearest—you, whose will should be law, to
whose judgment all must defer—would only say a
few words yourself, both on this subject and—"

"No, no!" interrupted Mr. Effingham quickly;
"these trifles do not lie within my province.   I make
it a rule never to interfere with these petty domestic
concerns.   You will consult with Lady Selina, and
then decide as seems best to yourself."

"Lady Selina!" murmured Clemence, in a tone
of disappointment; "oh, she never assists me at all

I should be rather inclined "—the young wife looked up playfully but timidly as she spoke—"to call her the leader of the Opposition!"

A slight frown passed across the brow of Mr. Effingham. He was by no means disposed to weaken, in any way, the connection of his family with a lady of rank and fashion, whose title gave a certain *éclat* to the establishment over which she so long had presided. The first time that the watchful eye of Clemence had ever perceived the slightest shade of displeasure towards her on the face of her husband was as he replied to her last observation,—

"I think, Clemence, that you do her injustice. Lady Selina is a woman of sense, and a great deal of experience in the world—one not in the least likely to be influenced by petty jealousies. I consider myself to be greatly indebted to her; and it is my wish that every member of my family should regard her in the same light that I do myself. As for little differences," he continued, rising from his seat and standing with his back to the fire, "the thousand trifles which make up the sum of domestic life, I desire to hear nothing, know nothing, of them. My mind is occupied with affairs more important, and in my own home, at least, I look for peace and repose."

It is possible that Mr. Effingham observed by the

fire-light something like glistening moisture on the downcast lashes of his wife; for, laying his hand kindly on her shoulder, he added in a gayer tone, "As long as my watch goes well, Clemence, I do not care to examine the works. I give you un-limited authority. Dissolve your whole House of Commons, if you please it; visit your peers with fine or imprisonment; but don't bring up appeals to me. A little time—a little judgment—they are all that is wanted; just act for the best, and take things easily."

Act for the best, and take things easily! How many times Clemence Effingham repeated to herself these oracular words! How long she pondered over the possibility of reconciling with each other the two clauses of the sentence! She had become the mis-tress of a mansion where everything, beyond mere externals, was in a state of woful neglect. Petty dishonesty was but one of the many evils which pre-vailed amongst the numerous members of the house-hold; while, in the family, selfishness, worldliness, and vanity reigned uncontrolled and scarcely dis-guised. It was a Gordian knot, indeed, that the young wife was given to untie, and she lacked strength to wield the conqueror's sword! Into the ear of her husband Clemence would have loved to have poured all her difficulties and trials; his sympathy and counsel might have removed many of the former, and cheered and encouraged her under the latter; but, occupied by other cares, Mr. Effingham left his young partner to bear her burden alone. Clemence made more than one attempt to avail herself of the experience of Lady Selina; but the woman of the world was cautious not to compromise herself, or in the slightest degree to share the unpopularity which is the almost inevitable fate of reformers. Nor was she inclined to own the existence of evils that had chiefly arisen from her own neglect. Lady Selina, when consulted by Clemence, listened to her with the cold, impassive smile which seemed the stereotyped expression of her unuttered opinion, "You are such a poor, inexperienced child!" Clemence was left to fight her battles quite alone.

But was it not possible to "take things easily" —to close her eyes to everything that it might be disagreeable to see; to follow the example of Lady Selina, and let affairs take their own course; to enjoy the luxury, and brightness, and gaiety of her life, without examining too closely behind the scenes? Clemence was strongly tempted to do so—strongly tempted to swim with the tide; to fling from herself the burden of responsibility, and forget care in the pleasures of the hour.

It was well for her that she had not received a

kinder welcome into the family. Had the path of
Clemence been strewn with nothing but flowers, it
would have been a path much more fraught with
peril. The unkindness and coldness which daily
wounded her affectionate and sensitive spirit, were
like thorny hedges which fenced her in from wandering from the narrow way. Had the cup of life been
all sweetness, it is too probable that it might have
intoxicated ; Lady Selina and her nieces were unconsciously mixing with it a bitter but salutary medicine.
Safer, far safer is it to have the worldly as enemies
than as friends. Nothing, perhaps, is more calculated
to make a Christian walk carefully than the *un-
avoidable* companionship of those who dislike both
himself and his religion. He feels that he must not
disgrace his profession—that he must give no handle
to the sharp blade of detraction, no occasion for the
enemy to blaspheme. His trials drive him to the
footstool of grace ; and while his patience and spirit
of forgiveness find constant exercise, the evil from
which he suffers makes him more keenly appreciate,
more earnestly desire, the harmony, holiness, and
happiness of heaven !

CHAPTER V.

THE circle of Mr. Effingham's acquaintance was large, and even in the dull wintry season Clemence found that the claims of society took up much of her time and attention. Knocks were frequent at her door; numerous visitors came to introduce themselves to the young wife of the wealthy banker. Clemence felt at first embarrassed, then amused, then wearied by that which lost its charm with its novelty. She became tired of ringing changes on the weather, the last new book, political prospects, and the movements of the court, with a succession of wearers of velvet bonnets and furred mantillas, whom she scarcely knew even by name. Clemence had not as yet much of the small change of conversation, and she had not the courage to produce her gold. Mrs. Effingham seldom entered her carriage, which was usually at the disposal of Lady Selina; Clemence being well pleased to purchase, by relinquishing the luxury of a drive, a little respite from the oppressive companionship of the earl's daughter.

At Mr. Effingham's desire, Clemence, early in December, issued cards of invitation for that most formal, and, to a young housewife, most formidable of entertainments—a grand dinner party. She was almost ashamed to find how much her thoughts were occupied by earthly cares, how large a share of her anxious attention was given to preparations for an event of such comparatively trivial importance. Lady Selina, indeed, regarded such arrangements as part of the chief business of life, and did her best to wind up to nervous anxiety Clemence's desire to order all things so as to do credit to her husband's establishment. The favourite topic of Lady Selina now appeared to be the strange mistakes, the unpardonable blunders which had occurred within, and far beyond, the limits of her experience, at parties given by the uninitiated. She also delighted to expatiate on such qualities in the expected guests as might render them formidable to their young hostess. Lord Vaughan was a connoisseur in the culinary art, and paid an unheard-of salary to his French cook ; Lady Praed always detected at a glance the smallest error in matters of form ; Colonel Parsons and Sir William Page were keen opponents in politics, and it would require much tact and management on the part of Mrs. Effingham to ward off any unpleasant discussion. Clemence listened, sighed, and heartily wished that the dreaded evening were over.

Then serious cares disturbed her. The more the young wife entered into the details of her establishment, the more she became aware of the difficulties which surrounded her at every step. Her servants appeared in a combination to overreach and deceive her. Every effort to introduce greater order and economy into her household was met with dogged opposition, and Mrs. Ventner resented all interference on the part of her mistress as a personal injury. The annoyance which Clemence had to endure from the members of her family was of a more painful nature. Arabella and Louisa never forgot—their aunt would never have suffered them to forget—that if Mrs. Effingham was placed above them by marriage, by birth she was not their equal. Clemence, inexperienced as she was, had sufficient natural powers of observation to detect the radical errors in the education of the daughters of her husband. But while she perceived the evil, she sought in vain for its cure; and the joyous hopes with which she had commenced her married life, like the fabled wings of Icarus melting in the sultry beams of the sun, no longer bore her buoyantly aloft!

It is, perhaps, only those who have known little of common cares who can smile on them as a trifling burden. To the young and the sensitive, who have hitherto trodden earth almost as free from petty anxieties as the bird on the wing, or the blossom on the tree, the sudden pressure of new responsibilities is sometimes almost overwhelming. They could better endure hardship and pain ; human compassion might then bring them relief, and they would more fully realize the blessed consolations of religion. And yet, is the command which embodies a precious privilege—the command to cast all our cares upon One who careth for us—limited only to that class of trials which man recognizes as afflictions? All earthly events in the sight of our Great Master must appear in themselves to be but trifles ; but when connected with their effects upon immortal beings, when made a means to train and discipline souls, the merest trifles assume weight and importance. A teacher's anxieties, a housewife's cares, the responsibilities of the mistress of an establishment, seem of too trivial and uninteresting a nature even for the light pages of a fiction ; but yet they, in the history of thousands and tens of thousands, form " the sum of human things." A decisive battle may be fought even in the narrow limits of a home. Solomon prayed for wisdom from above to direct aright the affairs of a kingdom ; the same wisdom in kind, though not in degree, is required by the humblest matron who would rule her household in the fear of God ; and where Solomon sought, she must seek it.

"I could wish that I were ten years older !" said Clemence to herself, as, seated in a large arm-chair, she nervously awaited the appearance of a servant whose conduct had given just subject for displeasure, and to whom she felt it necessary to administer rebuke. "I almost think that Vincent and I would enjoy life more in some country cottage, with just one maid to attend on us, away from all this grandeur and state, contented and happy in each other. Money does not seem worth all the care and trouble that it brings. I was much merrier last Christmas time, when, with my well-filled basket on my arm, I trod over the crisp snow on my way from cottage to cottage, sure of a welcome everywhere from lips that would not flatter and hearts that would not deceive ! I have, perhaps, larger means of usefulness here, but not of that kind of work which would most warm and gladden my own spirit ! It is pleasanter to build up than to pull down—to do good than to oppose evil—to serve God by winning blessings from man, than to serve Him by drawing on one's self the anger and dislike of others. But what is clear duty must be done, whether it be painful or pleasant.

We are not left to choose our own work, but we must trust to be given strength to perform it bravely."

A few days before the one fixed upon for the party, Mr. Effingham left Belgrave Square for a short period upon business. It was Clemence's first separation from her husband since their marriage, and she felt that during his absence all the sunshine of her life would be gone. To have been left quite alone would have been less painful; it was far worse than solitude to be left with her step-daughters and Lady Selina.

The haughty shyness which Arabella and Louisa had at first displayed before Mrs. Effingham had entirely worn away. They rather now, at least while their father was absent, made a parade of their perfect ease, and on the evening preceding his return chatted together with Mademoiselle Lafleur, as if scarcely aware of their step-mother's presence. Clemence sat quietly at her work, a pained listener to a flow of folly and gossip. Lady Selina appeared to be dozing in her arm-chair before the fire.

At length the conversation turned upon the clergyman whose ministry the family regularly attended— an earnest, good, but eccentric man. Arabella began turning him into ridicule, to the great amusement of her sister and governess, but the indignation of Mrs. Effingham.

"He ought to be elected preacher to the blind," laughed Louisa; "it would be so much better not to be able to see him!"

"They would make him over to the deaf and dumb," rejoined her sister; "for it would be better still not to be able to hear him!"

Clemence felt that she should no longer keep silence—she felt that she was bound to bear her witness to what was right in the presence of the children of her husband; and yet, reluctant as she was to give pain or offence, her reproof was couched in the mildest language, and uttered in the most gentle tone.

"Do you not think, dear Arabella," said the step-mother, "that when we listen to the preaching of the Word, it is rather upon the message than the messenger that we should fix our earnest attention?"

It was the first time that Clemence Effingham had ventured on anything approaching to a rebuke to her step-daughters. Her words, so strongly contrasting with the tone of the preceding conversation, had the effect of instantaneously silencing it; and such an uncomfortable stillness succeeded that Clemence at last felt herself forced to break it.

"I think that I must propose a little sociable reading," she said, "to make the evenings pass pleasantly while my husband is away. It will give us subjects to think of and talk over. I remember that my dear father used often to say that it is far safer and better, as a general rule, to converse about *things* than about *persons*."

"Had his unfortunate patients to take his precepts as well as his physic?" cried Arabella, with a pert insolence which was intended to "put down" the first attempt of her step-mother to interfere with her perfect freedom.

If Lady Selina was asleep, her dreams must have been of a pleasing nature, for they called up a smile on her face. Louisa and mademoiselle glanced at each other, and then at Mrs. Effingham, to see how the insult would be taken.

A burning flush rose to the cheek of Clemence,— she had been touched in a most tender part; not that she was so keenly sensible to the allusion to her own humble parentage intended to be conveyed in the flippant remark, but anything like disrespect to the memory of her venerated father stung her to the quick. Her heart glowed with angry resentment; it was with a painful effort that she repressed the expression of it. Clemence paused for a few seconds till she could speak calmly, then, with a quiet dignity, said, "Arabella Effingham, you appear scarcely to recollect that you address yourself to the wife of your father."

Arabella started from her seat, and hastily left the room, shutting the door violently behind her. Not another word was spoken for some time in the drawing-room, and Louisa and her governess took the first opportunity of quietly following Arabella, and leaving Mrs. Effingham to that which was ever to her most depressing—a *tête-à-tête* with Lady Selina.

"She has thrown down the gauntlet! she has chosen to commence the war!" exclaimed Arabella, as, pacing up and down her room, with all her proud spirit flashing from her eyes, she poured out her indignation to her sister and mademoiselle. "If she expects that she's to rule and dictate here, she'll find herself very much mistaken; the daughters of Lady Arabella Effingham never will bow to the control of the orphan of an apothecary!"

"We must take care, though, that we do not bring ourselves to grief," said Louisa, who was, if not more cautious, yet less irritable by nature; "she has papa's ear, and may set him against us. I dare say she's as spiteful as a toad—those meek, sanctified creatures always are!"

Clemence went early to her own room, but it was very long before she retired to rest. Her spirits were fluttered and agitated. In vain had been all her efforts to conciliate, all her attempts to win for herself the affections of her husband's daughters. She saw stretching before her, in endless perspective, a prospect of disunion and dissension, proud insolence and malicious enmity. Clemence leaned her brow on her clasped hands, and the hot tears trickled slowly down her cheeks, as she repeated to herself the words of the wise king: *Better is a dinner of herbs where love is, than a stalled ox and hatred therewith.*

"And how will it all end?" she murmured. "Is it not hard that I, who never willingly offended a human being, should be the object of such determined dislike, should find hatred where I proffer love, and be regarded as an enemy by those whom I would sacrifice much to serve? Is it not hard?" —the words died upon her lips, a feeling of self-reproach arose in the young wife's breast. What was she, that she should look for exemption from the common lot of her Master's followers? Had she any right to murmur under the pressure of a daily cross? *Hard!*—and had it ever been promised that life should be all softness and enjoyment? Would it not be folly to expect it? would it not be cowardice to desire it? If the Christian, overlooking second causes, fix his thoughts on an all-directing Providence, he will see how that Providence, working by earthly means, makes even the unkindness that wounds, and the malice that injures, important aids in forming the characters of the heirs of glory. It was from the elements of chaos that God drew forth a world of beauty; and some of His children's fairest virtues spring, as it were, from the evil around them. Patience could not have birth in heaven, nor forgiveness in the society of angels; without opposition Christian firmness could not appear, nor without trials be shown resignation.

Clemence pondered over the words, *If ye love them which love you, what reward have you? do not even the publicans the same?* and a clearer light than had ever been granted to her before fell on the command, *Love your enemies*—that divine command, enforced by a divine Example, and requiring divine aid to fulfil. Her hopes of overcoming the prejudices of her husband's family were now becoming faint; but a nobler hope had succeeded—the hope of overcoming her own feelings of resentment towards them, and of pleasing her heavenly Master by a meek endeavour to fulfil His will. Were not the hearts of all in His hands?

While Arabella and Louisa were revolving schemes of opposition, and their aunt was secretly rejoicing in the disunion, which had chiefly resulted from her own malicious efforts, Clemence knelt down and earnestly, fervently prayed in the silence of her chamber. Nor prayed she alone for herself, or the husband dearer than self, but separately and by name for each of the members of her family. If the prayer was not answered for all, was it not returned in blessings into her own bosom—the blessing of that peace in the heart which is even more priceless than peace in the home?

CHAPTER VI

A DECIDED MOVE.

RABELLA marked with secret satisfaction on the following morning the weary looks of her youthful step-mother; she regarded them as a favourable token of her own success in what she called "the war of independence." Following up what she considered to be her advantage, Arabella treated Mrs. Effingham at breakfast with marked discourtesy and neglect; would not even reply to her morning salutation, but preserved a proud silence throughout the whole of the meal. Clemence was pained by her manner, but outwardly took no notice of it.

In the afternoon, to the joy of his wife, Mr. Effingham returned to his home. The quick eye of affection soon detected that he looked graver, more thoughtful and careworn, than before he had quitted London. Doubtless he was wearied by his journey, and with tender consideration Clemence attended to

everything that might promote his comfort. "I
will vex him with none of my own little troubles,"
was her inward resolution; "if clouds will gather
without, all must be sunshine for him at least within
his own little home-circle."

So, when they were alone together, Clemence
again assumed the gaiety of a child, and, shunning
painful themes, amused her husband by a description of the little housewifely devices and arrangements which she had formed during his absence,
especially in reference to her first dinner party.
She told him how she had planned this, and discovered that, during long and serious colloquies
with Mrs. Ventner; she made him laugh at her
own blunders and mistakes, but assured him of her
resolve that, in the face of all difficulties, her first
entertainment should prove *"un grand succès !"*

"And yet, after all, Vincent," she exclaimed,
taking his hand within both her own, "I do not
think that I was ever intended to play a dis-
tinguished part in the great world! All these
elaborate preparations for a few hours' amusement
seem, to my unsophisticated mind, like making an
iron strong-box to enclose a bubble. We take every
precaution to prevent accident—rack invention to
make our pleasure secure—fasten it in with golden
padlock and key;—in a short space we look in to

see what has become of it, and lo ! the bubble has vanished into thin air, or," she added, laughing, " been metamorphosed into a heap of ugly bills ! If what we seek in entertaining be simply to give enjoyment, a party of children in a strawberry-bed will succeed much better, I suspect, in finding it, than all our grandee guests to-morrow over their turtle, venison, and champagne. I know that I, for one, would much rather lead the party amongst the strawberries. I should hardly find courage to sit at the head of that formidable table, between an erudite lord and a satirical baronet, but for re-membering who presides at the other end. O Vincent ! how little have outward circumstances to do with real, solid enjoyment ! Your presence gives an interest and zest to the pleasures which wealth may procure ; but that presence would suffice to make me happy even in the midst of poverty."

The thoughts of Mr. Effingham had wandered while Clemence was speaking ; his eyes were fixed, not upon her, but upon the fire, as if watching the little gas-jets which caught fire for a moment, burned vividly, and then were suddenly extinguished in smoke. But the last word which his wife had uttered struck his ear, and jarred like a discord upon it.

" Poverty !" he repeated quickly, " you never

will, never can know it. I have just settled sixty
thousand pounds on you, Clemence, in case — in
case of anything happening to me."

Clemence raised her head, and silently thanked
him by a look of grateful love, then pressed his
hand to her lips. Could Mr. Effingham have read
the thought which passed through his young wife's
mind, he would have seen it instinctively form itself
into a prayer that she never might survive her beloved
husband to benefit by this new proof of his affection.

The long *tête-à-tête* held in the study filled
Arabella's mind with considerable alarm. Louisa's
warning recurred to her with unpleasant vividness,
and she dwelt on the idea until she became certain
that her step-mother would try to influence her
father against her, and perhaps act the part of the
cuckoo nestling towards the unfortunate little hedge-
sparrows.

Notwithstanding the pride which made her "defy
the malice of any low-born intruder," Arabella's
relief was considerable when, on Mr. and Mrs.
Effingham rejoining the family, not even her jealous
suspicion could detect the slightest alteration in her
father's manner towards her. "She has not com-
plained of me, after all," thought Arabella. "Well,
that is more than I expected." She might have
added, " More than I deserved."

It was, perhaps, some slight feeling of obligation to Clemence for her forbearance, or, more probably, a little natural prudence, that now occasioned an improvement in the demeanour of the two girls towards Mrs. Effingham, though Arabella never dreamed of stooping to offer an apology for her former impertinence. Clemence rejoiced at the change, though she doubted its motive, and, by cordial kindness and winning attention, sought to follow up her advantage. After breakfast the next morning, Clemence, laying her hand affectionately on the shoulder of Louisa, proposed that she should accompany her to her Parnassus, as she playfully called the school-room. Mademoiselle Lafleur had gone for a few weeks to spend her Christmas holidays with some friends, and Mrs. Effingham looked upon the time of her absence as a favourable opportunity to draw her husband's daughters more closely to her by mingling more in their occupations and amusements. Clemence was also anxious to be better acquainted with their usual routine of life; for the more she had seen and known of their governess, the more she distrusted her as a guide of youth.

"I think that this room would be more comfortable with curtains," observed Clemence; "and you really require a nice little book-case on this table. What a delightful piano!" and she ran her fingers lightly over the keys. "Louisa, you and I must have many a duet together; I do so delight in music."

Then the drawings of Arabella were examined; and if the praise of Clemence was less profusely garnished with superlatives than that of mademoiselle had been, it carried on it more of the stamp of sincerity. Mrs. Effingham had a correct eye, and a taste for art, though she had had little opportunity of cultivating it; and the pleasure and interest with which she looked over the portfolio were gratifying to the haughty Arabella.

"And what may this beautiful book be?" inquired Clemence, laying her hand upon a volume bound in pink and gold.

"That is my album," replied Louisa; "it is to be filled with original poetry. I hope that you will write in it some day, Mrs. Effingham;" and as Clemence smiled and shook her head, Louisa added, "You will at least answer the three questions at the end of the book;" and she turned over rapidly to the place where, at the head of three separate columns, were written three sentences: WHAT IS HAPPINESS? WHAT IS MISERY? WHAT DO YOU MUCH WISH FOR?

Clemence glanced down the page with an amused eye, reading a most heterogeneous collection of descriptions of the various pleasures and pains of mankind. She needed not the initials at the end of each written opinion to guess who had penned to the three questions the following replies :—

DISTINCTION; OBSCURITY; A NAME.—A. E.
A FANCY-BALL; SMALL-POX; AN OPERA-BOX.—L. E.

"I must have you write, I am so curious to know what you think!" exclaimed Louisa, dipping a pen in the bronze ink-stand which stood on the table.

Clemence had neither the affectation which requires urgent entreaties, nor the vanity which refuses to do anything which it is not certain to do well. She reflected for a few seconds, then under the questions—WHAT IS HAPPINESS? WHAT IS MISERY? WHAT DO YOU MUCH WISH FOR? wrote,—

UNISON; DISCORD; HARMONY.

"I see little variety in unison and harmony," said Arabella coldly; "it is what papa would call a distinction without a difference."

"Does it seem so to you?" replied Mrs. Effingham. "I tried to condense into three words the sentiment contained in the verse, —

> ' Judge not thy differing brother, nor in aught
>   Condemn; his prayer and thine may rise above,
> Though mingling not in *unison of thought*,
>   Yet blending in the harmony of love.'

We cannot have here below that perfect *unison* in

all things which will form part of the happiness of heaven; but *harmony*, peace, concord may exist even between those whose opinions and tastes are dissimilar; and that," she added, with a cordial smile, "is what I most ardently 'wish for.'"

"Fire and water can never agree together," muttered Arabella to herself, in a tone too low to reach the ear of her step-mother, though Clemence saw the expression on the proud girl's face, which needed no words to convey its meaning. Not choosing to take open notice of the look, Mrs. Effingham turned to another part of the book, in which selections of poetry were written in various hands. One brief piece arrested her eye (it was written in the French language), and an unwonted shade of displeasure passed over her countenance as she read it.

"This is worse than levity," observed Clemence very gravely; "how could such lines have found entrance into your book?" And turning the leaf, she marked the name "Antoinette Lafleur" at the end of the piece.

"Oh! mademoiselle calls that a *jeu d'esprit!* She thinks it remarkably clever; but she did not compose it herself," added Louisa quickly, for she met Clemence's glance of indignant surprise; "she copied it out of this book; it is a book that she raves about."

"Have you ever read it?" inquired Mrs. Effing-ham.

"Just parts of it. Mademoiselle only lent it to us last week; but she says that it is the first book in the language."

"I have heard of it, though I have never perused it, never seen it before," said Clemence, retaining the volume in her grasp. She knew it to be the work of a famous infidel writer, who so mingled wit with blasphemy, that the brilliancy of his style, like the phosphorescent light which sometimes gleams from corruption, gave strange attraction to opinions re-pugnant alike to morality and religion.

Clemence made no further observation to her step-daughters on the subject while she remained in the school-room; but on quitting it she descended at once, with the book in her hand, to Mr. Effing-ham's study. "This is no trifling matter," she thought, "to be lightly passed over and forgotten; this is no little personal concern which I should forbear intruding on the attention of my husband. This unhappy woman may for years have been undermining the principles of his daughters, and I should wrong him were I to withhold from him the knowledge which I have providentially obtained."

Mr. Effingham had not that morning gone, as was his wont, to his banking-house in the city. Cle-

mence found him in his study, and with a few
words to explain where and how she had discovered
it, she placed the poisonous work of the infidel
author before him.

Mr. Effingham had been a careless, although an
affectionate father. With his family, as with his
household, he had been content to believe that all
was right, if he saw nothing very glaringly wrong.
He had been imbued deeply with the idea that
making money was the main business of man's life;
and the regulation of his establishment, the education of his children, the training of immortal souls,
he had quietly left to others. He was, however,
full of reverence for religion; he wished his children
to be brought up in the same, though his efforts to
secure that end had not gone far beyond the mere
wish. He was as much startled at the idea of
infidel doctrines being instilled into the unsuspicious
minds of his young daughters, as if he had seen a
serpent coiling beside the pillow on which they
were sleeping. He was more aware of the perilous
nature of the book than his wife could be, who had
known it only by report. Mr. Effingham's usually
placid nature was roused into stern indignation.

"Never shall that woman set her foot across my
threshold again!" he exclaimed, striking his hand
upon the volume. "I have never liked her—never

THE FRENCH BOOK.

Page 64

felt confidence in her; with her soft, cat-like manner, she always gave me the impression of claws being concealed beneath the velvet! Write to her at once, Clemence, and dismiss her; I will give you a cheque to enclose. And send away that detestable book; the only fit place for it is the back of the fire!"

Clemence obeyed, and with a thankful heart. It seemed to her that by the dismissal of Mademoiselle Lafleur, one of the heaviest obstructions in her own path had been suddenly and unexpectedly removed. She had felt it almost a hopeless endeavour to influence her step-daughters for good, while her efforts were secretly, insidiously counteracted by one with whom they were in daily familiar intercourse; yet without some definite cause, some obvious reason, Clemence would have shrunk from dismissing the governess chosen by Lady Selina, and favoured by her nieces. So bold a step would be certain to raise such a storm! The imagination of the youthful step-mother now rapidly built up for itself a bright castle in the air, founded on the hope that mademoiselle's place might be supplied by some woman of high principles and sterling worth, who would go hand in hand with herself in every plan for improvement. Clemence did not blind her eyes to the fact that her own unpopularity would almost assuredly be shared by any governess whom she

might select ; that Lady Selina's penetration would
be certain to discover faults in an angel ; and that
Arabella, if not Louisa also, would meet the stranger
at first with determined dislike.　But at Clemence's
age hope is strong; and one difficulty overcome seems
an earnest that all others will be removed.　Young
Vincent, too, was expected home the next day, and
Clemence looked forward with pleasure to a meeting
with one in whom she saw the image of his father.
Her spirit felt lighter and more joyous than it had
done ever since her first cold reception in Belgrave
Square.

Mrs. Effingham despatched her letter to Mademoiselle Lafleur, after showing it to her husband for
his approval ; but it was resolved, by his advice, to
say nothing on the subject to the family till the
ordeal of her grand entertainment should be over.

CHAPTER VII.

THE DINNER PARTY.

T still wanted twenty minutes to the hour appointed in the cards of invitation, but the toilet of Mrs. Effingham was already concluded, and after a somewhat anxious examination into what her husband would have termed "the machinery" of her establishment, now to be brought to its first formidable test, she entered her superb drawing-room, there to await her guests. The apartment was dimly lighted by a single pair of candles at the further end ; the crystal chandelier suspended from the ceiling, the ormolu candelabra on the mantel-piece, had not yet been kindled into sparkling constellations ; but the arrangement of every article of furniture was faultless, and the young mistress glanced around her with a feeling of pleasure, not, perhaps, unmingled with a little pride.

"O Mrs. Effingham, I am so glad that you have come !" exclaimed Louisa, advancing towards her with almost a dancing step, in a flutter of muslin and lace. "Here is a little note which came for you about five minutes ago; I dare say that it is an excuse from one of the guests."

Clemence broke the seal, and glanced over the contents. "You are right; Dr. Howard has been suddenly summoned to see a patient in the country."

"Oh! then, dear Mrs. Effingham," cried Louisa eagerly, laying her white-gloved hand on the arm of her step-mother, "you know that some one must fill his place; do—do let me go down to dinner!"

"Arabella is the elder," replied Clemence.

"Arabella!" repeated Louisa, pettishly; "there is very little difference between our ages, and I am the taller of the two; besides," she added more slowly, as if measuring her words as she spoke—"besides, after what passed the day before yesterday, I should hardly have expected you to favour Arabella."

"I should think it very wrong to favour either," said Clemence gravely, "and still more wrong to neglect either; for—" here she was suddenly interrupted and startled by the sound of a loud knock at the door.

"A guest already!" exclaimed Louisa, hurriedly attempting to pull on her left-hand glove.

"A guest already!" echoed Clemence, glancing uneasily at the unlighted chandelier, and laying her hand on the bell-rope.

In two minutes a loud voice was heard below in the hall. "Not see me!—going to have company! Trash and nonsense, man! she'll see me at any hour, and in any company!" and a heavy, tramping step immediately sounded on the stair, while Clemence exclaimed, with mingled pleasure, surprise, and vexation, "Oh! can it be my dear Uncle Thistlewood?" and hastening down the long room, she met him just as he flung the door wide open.

In a moment she was in his arms! The old sea-captain kissed his niece heartily, again and again, each time making the room resound. Louisa, extremely diverted, perhaps a little maliciously so, at what she considered the inopportune appearance of one of Mrs. Effingham's vulgar relations, advanced towards the door to have a nearer view of the meeting, and so came in for her share of it.

"Ah! one of your daughters, Clemence?" cried her old uncle, and he immediately bestowed on the astonished Louisa a fatherly salute. "Fine, well-grown girl," he continued in his loud, cheerful voice; "must make you feel quite old, my darling, to have children as tall as yourself! But let us have a little of the fire, for it's blowing great guns to-night, and I've had my feet half frozen off on the top of the omnibus!" And marching up to the grate at the end of the room, the captain spread out his coarse

red hands to the warmth, after having stirred the
fire to a roaring blaze, and stamped on the rug to
warm his feet, leaving the impression of his boots on
the velvet. "And now, let me have a better look
of your sweet face, blessings on it!" cried the sea-
man, turning towards Clemence, and taking hold of
both her hands, while he fixed on her a gaze of fond
admiration. Very lovely, indeed, looked Mrs. Effingham, with the flush of excitement on her cheek, and
the sparkle of affection in her eye. Captain Thistlewood was evidently pleased with his survey, though
he said,—

"You seem to me a little older and thinner than
when we parted, May-blossom, and you looked just
as well in your good russet gown as in that dainty
blue velvet with the sparklers; but you'll do very
well—do very well! And now I dare say that you
want to know what brought the old man gadding
here." He threw himself into an arm-chair to converse more at ease, perfectly regardless of the presence of the servants, now engaged in illuminating
the room.

"You see, ever since you left us, Stoneby's grown
as dull as ditch-water—all the life seems gone out
of it. Parson's always busy as usual—too busy to
have much time to give to a little social gossip;
and his wife's sick, and keeps her room in the cold

weather. There's nothing stirring in the village, or for ten miles round—the very windmill seems to have gone to sleep; and the robins, to my mind, don't chirp and sing as they used to do. Susan has taken it into her silly head to marry, like her mistress, and the new girl don't suit me—breaks my crockery, and over-roasts my mutton. The long and short of it is, that home is not home without my May-blossom. I bore it as long as I could—lonely evenings and all. At last says I to myself, 'I'll put up my bundle and be off to London. I know there's some one there will be glad to see the old man ; let him arrive when he may, he won't be unwelcome !' "

Clemence felt indignant with herself for not being able more fully and cordially to respond to her uncle's assurance. " The world must indeed have already exercised its corrupting influence over me," was her silent reflection, " when I can experience anything but joy at the sound of that dear familiar voice ! But what will my husband say ? " As the thought crossed her mind, the door opened, and Mr. Effingham entered the room.

A greater contrast could scarcely be imagined than that between the tall, dignified, handsome gentleman, with his polished manner and graceful address, and the short, square-built, jovial old captain, with a face much of the shape and colour-

ing, without the smoothness, of a rosy-cheeked
apple.   Mr. Effingham was aware of the arrival of
Thistlewood—indeed, no one in the house, not
afflicted with deafness, was likely to be altogether
ignorant of it ; he was therefore quite prepared for
the meeting.   To the unspeakable relief of Clemence, Mr. Effingham cordially held out his hand to
the sailor, who shook it as he might have worked a
pump handle, and then said in a kindly voice, " I
am glad to see you, captain ; you must take up your
quarters with us."

Thistlewood nodded in acquiescence, as one who
felt an invitation to be quite an unnecessary form ;
but Clemence's expressive eyes were turned on her
husband with a look of gratitude, which told how
much it was appreciated by her.

" We expect company this evening," continued
Mr. Effingham.

" Ay, so the white-headed chap with the gold
cable told me."

" It does not want a quarter of an hour to dinner-
time," said the gentleman, taking out his watch.

" Dinner-time ! I should rather call it supper-
time.   Ha ! ha ! ha ! I dined before one, but my
long journey has made me rather peckish.   A beef-
steak wouldn't come anyways amiss."

" You may like to make some little alteration in

your dress," observed Mr. Effingham, glancing at the pea-jacket and muddy boots of his guest; "my servant will show you your apartment."

The question of toilet was evidently one of supreme indifference to the honest captain; a dress good enough to walk in seemed to him to be good enough to eat in; but he made no difficulty about compliance. He was just about to quit the room, when it was entered by Arabella.

The young lady stared at the rough-looking stranger with an air of haughty inquiry which would have abashed a sensitive man; but Captain Thistlewood was as little troubled with shyness as with hypochondria—his nerves were weather-proof, as well as his constitution—his perceptions were blunt to ridicule or insult, if only directed against himself.

"Ha! another fine daughter!" he exclaimed; "we must not meet as strangers, my dear;" and he would have greeted Arabella in the same paternal style as her sister, but for the backward step and the indignant look, which might have beseemed an empress.

"Who is this man?" she exclaimed.

"Mrs. Effingham's uncle and my friend," was her father's reply, uttered in a tone which effectually repressed for the time any further expression of Arabella's scorn.

The two girls retired to the back drawing-room to converse together, Louisa full of mirth, Arabella of indignation; while Clemence, glad to be a few minutes alone with her husband, laid her hand fondly on his arm, and murmured, "How good you have been to me, Vincent!"

"I could wish that your uncle had not arrived till to-morrow," said Mr. Effingham; "but I could not but treat with courtesy and kindness him from whose hand I received my wife. Will there be room at the table?"

"Yes; Dr. Howard has declined."

"To which lady would you introduce Captain Thistlewood?"

"Let me consider," said Clemence, thoughtfully; "who is most good-natured and quiet? Uncle sometimes says such strange things."

"What say you to Miss Mildmay?"

"She would show no rudeness at least, but—" here the conversation was interrupted by the entrance of servants.

When the little captain re-appeared in the drawing-room, radiant in blue coat, buff waistcoat and brass buttons, most of the guests had arrived. That semicircle of ladies had been formed which presents to the eye of a hostess as formidable a front as the unbroken square of infantry, bristling with steel, does to an opposing general. Mrs. Effingham was, as yet, entirely unskilled in the art of mixing together the various materials of society. With a shy, anxious air, she glided from one guest to another to accomplish the necessary form of introduction, —to her a serious undertaking, especially as some of her visitors were strangers to her. Clemence tried to forget that the cold, criticizing eye of Lady Selina was watching her every movement, and sought to remember only, that even in the arrangement of a party she might please her husband, and do credit to him. The entrance of Captain Thistlewood had considerable effect in breaking the ice of formality which lies like a crust upon London society, though in a manner that astonished the guests, and embarrassed the master and mistress of the house. The jovial sailor was as much at his ease in the polished circle as amidst shipmates round a cuddy table; and his loud voice and merry laugh, as he stood with his thumbs in his pockets, chatting with Louisa, created an unusual sensation.

"Who may that lively old gentleman be?" inquired Lord Vaughan of Lady Selina.

"One of Mrs. Effingham's near relations," was her distinctly audible reply.

Clemence hastened to introduce the captain to Miss Mildmay, in hopes that that lady's opposite

qualities might serve as a kind of compensation
balance, to moderate her uncle's boisterous mirth.
Miss Mildmay was a sallow lady on the shady side
of forty, attired in a pale sea-green silk, with long,
lank sprays of artificial leaves drooping low on each
side of her head. She was a mild, inanimate sample
of gentility, whose very eyes seemed to have had
the colour washed out of them, and whose prim,
pursed-up lips rarely unclosed to speak, and still
more rarely to smile. Miss Mildmay was one of the
dead-weights of society, and was, therefore, judi-
ciously coupled with the little, noisy, bustling captain, who, like some steam locomotive, would sturdily
puff straight on his way, regardless of obstacles,
unconscious of observation, ready to go over or
through an obstruction, but never to turn aside for
it, let it be what it might.

As Captain Thistlewood wanted nothing but a
listener, he dashed bravely along the railway of conversation, choosing, of course, his own lines—now
on country subjects, now on sea—turnips and tor-
nadoes, calves and Cape wines,—till, on dinner being
announced, he gallantly handed down his partner,
and in his simplicity took his seat near the top of
the table, in order to be, as he said, " within hail
of my niece."

Miss Mildmay languidly drew off her gloves ;

there was a pause of a few minutes in the conversation, for Captain Thistlewood, bending forward, was looking with curious eyes down the length of the table, decked out in the magnificence of modern taste. He had never seen anything like it before.

"I say!" he burst out at length, "do you call this a dinner? Nothing on the table but fruit, and flowers, and sweat-meats, that wouldn't furnish a meal for a sparrow!"

The sailor's exclamation overcame the gravity of several of those who sat near him; even Miss Mildmay put up her feather-tipped fan to her lips,—it is possible that it might be to conceal a smile.

"But what's that on the dish before us?" continued the captain, surveying it with curious surprise. "Peaches in December! I never heard of such a thing!" And determined to investigate the phenomenon more closely, he suddenly plunged his fork into the nearest peach, and carried it off to his plate. In a moment his knife had divided the sugared cake into halves. "It's all a sham!" he cried, pushing it from him; "no more a peach than I am!"—and then, for the first time in the experience of man, a little laugh was actually heard from Miss Mildmay, in which Clemence herself, who had seen the proceeding, could not refrain from joining. The captain laughed loudest of all, quite unconscious that anything excited mirth except the "sham" of the peaches.

"I did not know, Clemence," he cried, "that you would have been up to such dodges!" and the exclamation set his end of the table in a roar. Such a merry party had perhaps never before assembled round the mahogany in Belgrave Square.

Notwithstanding the prognostications of Lady Selina, nothing glaringly wrong appeared in the arrangements of the banquet. Perhaps the sharp eye of malice detected here and there some token of inexperience in the mistress of the feast, but few were disposed to criticize harshly. Lord Vaughan did not regret the absence of his French cook; and Colonel Parsons and Sir William Page sat as contentedly on the same side of the table, as if they had never occupied opposite benches in "The House." All would have proceeded in the most approved routine of formality and regularity, but for the presence of the merry old captain, who cut his jokes, and told his stories, and pledged his niece in a loud, jovial tone, to the great amusement of the guests, but the embarrassment of Mrs. Effingham.

Arabella and Louisa awaited the ladies in the drawing-room, where they were joined by Thistlewood and the other gentlemen. The stiff semicircle was again dashingly broken by the brave old captain, who chatted merrily with the laughing Louisa, proposed a country dance or a reel, and engaged her as his partner. But nothing so informally lively as an impromptu dance after dinner was to be thought of in Belgrave Square. The grand piano, indeed, was opened ; but it was that a succession of ladies, after a due amount of declining and pressing, might give the company the benefit of their music.

Captain Thistlewood was extremely fond of music, and therefore at once planted himself by the piano, beating time like a conductor. The concert opened with a bravura song from Miss Praed, to which he listened with much of the feeling which Johnson expressed when asked if a lady's performance were not wonderful : " Wonderful !—would it were *impossible !* " Then followed a languid "*morceau*" from Miss Mildmay, which the composer must have designed for a soporific ; and then Arabella seated herself before the instrument. Her forte was rapid execution ; hers was a hurry-skurry style of playing, hand over hand, the right suddenly plunging into the bass, then the left unexpectedly flourishing away in the treble—each seeming bent on invading the province of the other, and causing as much noise there as possible. As the performer finished with a crashing chord, the captain, who had been watching her fingers with great diversion, clapped Arabella

on the shoulder. "Well done, my lass!" he exclaimed; "that's what I should call a thunder-and-
lightning piece, stunning in both senses of the word!
But still, for my part, I like a little quiet tune;
— did you ever hear your mother sing 'Nelly
Bly'?"

Arabella looked daggers as she withdrew from the
piano. To be so treated, as if she were a child—
she, an earl's grand-daughter—before so many guests,
and by *him*, the vulgar little brother-in-law of an
apothecary; it was more than her proud spirit could
endure! Mrs. Effingham should pay dearly for the
insult!

Nothing further occurred to vary the monotony
of the fashionable London entertainment. The evening wore on, much after the usual style of such
evenings, till, one after another, the guests took
leave of their young bright hostess; and there was
cloaking in the ante-room, and bustle in the hall,
and rolling of carriages from the door—till at length
the lights in the drawing-room were darkened, silence
settled down even on the servants' hall, the grand
entertainment was concluded, the laborious trifle
ended, and that which had cost so much thought
and anxious care, to say nothing of trouble and
expense, passed quietly into the mass of nothings,
once important, which Memory, when she takes

inventory of her possessions, throws aside for ever as mere tarnished tinsel not worth the preserving.

"I am so glad that it is over!" thought Clemence.

CHAPTER VIII.

R. EFFINGHAM was always an early riser.
The next morning he was earlier than
usual, and had not only commenced his
breakfast, but concluded it, and gone off
to his business eastward, before any of
the ladies, except his wife, had made their
appearance in the breakfast-room. Want of punc-
tuality in her step-daughters was one of the evils
which Clemence longed, though in vain, to reform.
Lady Selina's example not only excused it, but rendered it in a certain degree fashionable in the family.
"It is for slaves to be tied down to hours!" exclaimed Arabella, on a gentle hint being once ventured by Clemence; "only dull mechanics, whose
time is their bread, count their minutes as they
would count their coppers!"

Clemence was not, however, Mr. Effingham's only
companion at his early meal. The jovial captain,

full of merriment and good-humour, and disposed to
do full justice to the ham and an unlimited number
of eggs, performed his part at the table. His niece
would have been extremely diverted by his *naïve*
observations on the events of the previous evening—
observations which showed at once natural shrewd-
ness and the most absolute ignorance of fashionable
life—had she not feared that his boisterous hearti-
ness of manner might be disagreeable to her husband.
Mr. Effingham was perfectly polite, but did not look
disposed to be amused. He appeared hardly to hear
the jokes of the captain, and hurried over his breakfast with a thoughtful, pre-occupied air.

Clemence's own mind was often wandering to the
subject of Mademoiselle Lafleur, and she contem-
plated with some uneasiness and fear the effect which
would be produced on her circle by the announce-
ment of that lady's dismissal. She also felt anxious
as to the footing on which her dear old relative
would stand in the proud family to which she had
been united by marriage. In him a new and very
vulnerable point seemed presented to the shafts of
malice which were constantly levelled at herself.
His very simplicity and unconsciousness of insult
made her doubly sensitive on his account, and many
a plan Clemence turned over in her mind for guarding
him from the well-bred rudeness which none knew

better than Lady Selina how to show to one whom she despised. Mrs. Effingham's reflections made her more silent and grave than had been her wont. "She is not such a good talker as she used to be," thought the old uncle; "nor such a good listener neither, for the matter of that!"

Captain Thistlewood found, however, both a ready talker and listener when Louisa entered the room. The young lady, if the truth must be confessed, regarded the merry old sailor as rather an acquisition to the circle. He noticed her much, and Louisa would rather have been censured than unnoticed; he amused her, and love of amusement was one of her ruling passions. She could laugh *with* him when he was present, and *at* him when he was absent. Louisa imagined herself a wit; and what so needful to a wit as a butt! Her morning greeting to him was given with an air of coquettish levity, which contrasted with Arabella's sullen silence, and Lady Selina's frigid politeness.

"And what did you think of our party, Captain Thistlewood?" inquired Louisa, as the old sailor gallantly handed to her the cup of chocolate which Clemence had prepared.

"Well, it was good enough in its way, only too many kickshaws handed about, and too many lackeys behind the table to whip off the plate from before

you, if you chanced to look round at a neighbour.
I must say that your London society is a stiff, formal
sort of thing. It reminds one of those swindling
pieces of goods which tradesmen pass off on the
unwary—all *dress*, you see, just stiffened and
smoothed to sell, and not to wear. Only give the
gentility a good hearty pull, and the powder flies up
in your face!"

"I suppose that yesterday was the first time that
he ever sat at a gentleman's table!" muttered Arabella inaudibly to herself; but the thought expressed
itself in her face.

"If there's any powder about that young lass it's
gunpowder!" thought the captain; "we may look
out for an explosion by-and-by—I see she's primed
for a volley. But I'll try a little conciliation for
May-blossom's sake—hang out a flag of truce. No
wonder that my poor child looks grave and pale;—
a pretty life she must have of it here, with an ice-
berg on the one side and a volcano on the other!"
All the more determined to draw Arabella into conversation, from marking her haughty reserve, Captain Thistlewood rested his knife and fork perpen-
dicularly on either side of his plate, and addressed
her across the table.

"We're coming near to Christmas now. I like
the merry old season, and I shall be glad to see for

once how Christmas is kept in London. I noticed
many a jolly dinner hanging up in the butchers' and
poulterers' shops as I passed along in the 'bus;
quite a sight they are, those shops—turkeys strung
on long lines, as though they were so many larks;
and huge joints of beef, that, for their size, might
have been cut from elephants! Glorious they look
in the flaring gas-light, decked out with whole
shrubberies of holly! Then the pretty little Christ-
mas-trees, hung with tapers and gim-cracks—they
pleased me mightily too; for, thinks I, there'll be
plenty of harmless fun, plenty of laughing young
faces round those trees, when the tapers are lighted!
I love to see children happy, and 'specially the children of the poor. Shall I tell you my notion of a
good Christmas-tree?" Arabella looked as though
she did not care to hear it, but the captain took it
for granted that she did. "I'd have a tree as big
as the biggest of those yonder in the Square, and
invite all the ragged little urchins far and near to
the lighting of the same. I'd have it hung, not
with sparkling thing-a-bobs, or sugar trash in funny
shapes, not even with sham peaches," he added,
laughing, "but with good solid joints of meat for
blossoms, and warm winter jackets for leaves; and
I'll be bound that every child would think my tree
the very finest that he ever had seen in his life.

Don't you call that uniting the ornamental with the useful ? "

"The idea shows so much elegance, so much refinement of taste," replied Arabella, with satirical emphasis, " that it will doubtless be instantly carried out by Mrs. Effingham."

There was something in the tone in which the name was pronounced which stung the old sailor as no personal rudeness to himself could have done. As a single word will sometimes suffice to rouse a whole train of associations, startle a host of ideas into life, the name "Mrs. Effingham," so pronounced by her step-daughter, conjured up before the warm-hearted old man a picture coloured indeed, by fancy, but not without an outline of truth. His sweet Clemence was not loved and valued in her home ; she, his darling, his heart's delight, was looked down upon by those who should have deemed it an honour to sun themselves in her smile! Such was the suspicion which flashed out into words of sudden indignation.

"Mrs. Effingham ! and pray who may she be ? I see here my niece, your father's wife, your mother by marriage ; but no one whom you or I can either speak or think of as 'Mrs. Effingham !'"

The most insolent in temper are usually those who have least courage to back their insolence.

Those who delight in wounding the sensitive and
brow-beating the timid, when they find their weapon
crossed by another, when they become aware that
their shafts may be returned on themselves, often
are the first to draw back from the contest so
wantonly provoked.   Arabella was startled into a
momentary confusion; and her opponent, who carried "anger as the flint bears fire," at once recovered
his usual temper.   The captain was aware that he
had given way to a burst that had been scarcely
called for by anything actually uttered; he had,
perhaps, been too ready to imagine an affront where
no such thing was intended.

"Forgive an old man's vehemence," he said
frankly; "I got my ideas in the last century, and
they may by this time be quite old-fashioned.
There are many, I take it, who scarcely know what
to call a step-mother at first, especially one so
young.   For once I think that the French have hit
on a better title than our own.   It must sound odd
enough applied to many; but here is a case where
belle-mère is quite appropriate,"—he glanced fondly
at his niece; then added, bowing gallantly to
Louisa, "and also the title of *belle-fille.*"

The thunder-cloud only gathered blacker on the
brow of Arabella, but Louisa tittered and gaily replied, "I have often wondered why our French

neighbours should make such a spell of marriage—
to turn connections on both sides into beauties,
brothers, old fathers, and all! I'll ask mademoiselle for the derivation of the term. By-the-
by," added Louisa, addressing Clemence, " on what
day does mademoiselle come back ? "

It was an unfortunate question at that moment.
The flush which rose to the cheek of Clemence, her
little pause before she replied, fixed every eye upon
her. The young wife felt like one about to fire a
train, when she answered, "Mademoiselle is not
coming back at all."

"Not coming back!" exclaimed both girls at
once. "Not coming back!" echoed Lady Selina,
in accents of unfeigned surprise. Clemence knew
that some explanation was required, and she gave
it, in a tone as firm as she could command. " Mr.
Effingham and I have, after due reflection, decided
on making a change. We have very sufficient rea-
sons, and I trust—-"

But the train had been fired indeed, and before
Clemence could finish her sentence there was an un-
mistakable explosion ! Not that the governess had
in reality attached to herself any one present, or
that her pupils actually looked upon her dismissal
as a personal misfortune ; but a good handle was
suddenly offered to the hand of malice,—"the war

of independence" had required its watchword and its martyr, and the maligned, persecuted mademoiselle served at once for both. Arabella's smothered indignation could now creditably boil over in wrath, and a torrent of invective burst forth, swelled by Louisa's passionate exclamations. But most formidable was the awful dignity with which Lady Selina rose from her seat, adding her broken sentences of calm indignation: "Strange, mysterious, incomprehensible proceeding!"—"Personal insult to myself!"—"One who had selected that lady on the highest recommendations, who for years had reposed the utmost confidence in that lady, and who had ever found her more than justify that trust, not to be consulted on a step so important!" The very dress of Lady Selina seemed to rustle and tremble with offended pride. How could the timid, sensitive Clemence stand her ground against such an overwhelming avalanche of opposition?

She had but one ally present, and her dread was lest he should come to her aid. The veins on the captain's forehead were growing very large and his cheek very red; he glanced hurriedly, and almost fiercely, from one assailant to the other, as a lion might when encompassed by the hounds, only doubting in which quarter to make his spring. But

none of the enemy awaited the attack; Lady Selina
and her nieces all quitted the apartment, to excite
each other to fiercer wrath against the household
tyrant, who had dared, by such an unwarrantable
act of independence, to bid defiance to the clique!

"If ever I heard anything like this!" exclaimed
Captain Thistlewood, striking the table with vehemence; "the insolence, the audacity of these
young shrews!—the malice of that cantankerous
old dame! You must be protected from them,
Clemence. I'll after and tell them—"

"O uncle, dear uncle, let them go!" exclaimed
Clemence, holding the captain's arm to prevent his
sudden exit from the room; "you cannot help me,
indeed you cannot; it will blow over, it will—"

"Blow over!" thundered the veteran, trying to
extricate himself from her hold; "such a tornado
may blow over indeed, but it will first blow you
out of your senses! I'm glad I came here—I'm
heartily glad. I'll not have you exposed to this;
I'll—"

"Uncle!" cried Clemence nervously, "any movement on your part would only make matters a thousand times worse. For my sake be calm—be com-
posed. There is nothing from which I so shrink as
quarrels and dissensions in the house. Let us have
peace—"

"Peace!" exclaimed the indignant captain; "lay down our arms—strike our flag to such viragoes as these! No; if your husband has not the spirit to keep these termagants in order—"

"If you would not make me miserable," cried Clemence, "leave me and Mr. Effingham to smooth and settle things by ourselves. You cannot imagine the evil that might arise from the interference even of one so kind, and good, and loving as yourself! Be persuaded, dear uncle, be persuaded; take no notice of what has occurred."

It was with considerable difficulty that Clemence succeeded to a certain degree in quieting the old man's excitement. She persuaded him at length to leave the house for a few hours, in order to visit some London sights, knowing well that the sailor's anger, though it might be warm, was never enduring. It was with a sense of real relief that she heard the hall door close behind him; and she earnestly hoped that he might find so much amusement that he would not return until Mr. Effingham had come back from his business in the city.

Before Clemence had had breathing time in which to recover from the excitement of the last painful scene, one of her footmen entered the room, with two envelopes on a silver salver. As Mrs. Effingham mechanically took them up, he informed her

CAPTAIN THISTLEWOOD.

Page 81.

that Mrs. Ventner wished to speak to her for a few minutes.

The interview it is unnecessary to describe. From the first hour that the housekeeper had discovered that she had not a mere puppet to deal with, that her mistress could overlook accounts and detect inaccuracies, from that hour she had made up her mind that the same house could not hold them both. Mrs. Ventner had plundered enough from her master, during Lady Selina's careless reign, to make her, as she believed, independent; and, knowing that her books would not bear the close scrutiny which had probably been only postponed till the party should be over, and perhaps alarmed by the tidings which had now spread through the house that mademoiselle had been dismissed at a moment's notice, she resolved to avoid sharing the same fate by anticipating it, and gave her young mistress warning.

Clemence received the communication, to outward appearance, with great composure, but her spirits were fluttered and her mind oppressed; and when she had sought the quiet of her own room, she sat for some time in an attitude of listless thought, before remembering to examine the contents of the envelopes which she had carried unopened in her hand.

Only bills—uninteresting bills ; and yet not so
uninteresting neither, or there would not be that
slight tremble in the fingers that grasp them, or
that faint line on the fair brow so smooth but a
minute before.   These are the milliner's and dressmaker's bills; and the courage of Clemence is
failing her, as she glances down the long line, and
sums up the amount again and again, with ever
lessening hope that there may be some error in the
calculation.   Clemence had no fixed allowance
assigned her ; but her husband, soon after their
marriage, had replenished her slender purse with a
sum so large, that it had appeared to her almost
inexhaustible.   Clemence had a generous heart, and
loved to give with a liberal hand.   She had ex-
pended money very freely upon others, before becoming aware how much her personal expenses were
now likely to exceed the narrow limits within which
they had hitherto been restrained.   She had, however, reserved what she had hoped would be sufficient
to defray the two bills now before her, the only ones
yet unpaid.   But the young girl, brought up in
rural seclusion and ignorance of the fashionable
world, had formed a most incorrect estimate of rich
velvet dresses, and mantillas trimmed with costly
fur, handkerchiefs edged with the delicate productions
of Mechlin or Brussels—beautiful trifles, upon which

luxury lavishes her gold so freely, and which yet
contribute so little to actual enjoyment. Clemence
had little more than sufficient money left to clear
her debt to the milliner; Madame La Voye's heavy
bill lay before her, a weight upon her conscience as
well as her spirits.

"What will Vincent think—my noble, generous-
hearted husband—when he knows of my folly and
selfish extravagance? Not three months married,
and already in debt, deeply in debt—in debt for
the mere vanities of dress! Oh! he never would
have deemed his wife capable of acting so unworthy
a part. How shall I confess to him that his liberality has led me into such extravagance—that his
trusting love has met with such a return! And he
has been looking anxious and careworn of late; the
thought has even crossed my mind that business
concerns may not be prospering—that he may be
uneasy as regards his affairs. Oh! if it should be
so, and if I—vain, weak, thoughtless—should have
added to his cares instead of lightening them!"
The idea was to Clemence almost unbearable; bitter
self-reproach added its keen pang to those of anxious
care and wounded feeling; and it was some time
before she could calm her agitated spirits, or look
her difficulties fairly in the face.

When Clemence quitted her apartment, she was

suddenly met on the staircase by young Vincent, who had reached home about an hour previously, though, absorbed in her own painful reflections, she had not noticed the sound of an arrival. A joyful exclamation of welcome was on her lips, but her first glance at the face of the boy was sufficient to check its utterance. Giving her a look, in which dislike, scorn, and defiance were mingled, Vincent brushed past his step-mother without saying a word. And this was the son whom her heart had learned already to love—the son on whom she had built such hopes—in whose countenance she had traced such a resemblance to his father—who bore his name, and, as she trusted, would bear his character—the only member of her husband's family who had given her anything approaching to a welcome. The disappointment came at a moment when the spirit of Clemence was wounded by unkindness and depressed by self-reproach. This last drop of bitterness made her cup overflow. She returned to her own room with a hurried step, and throwing herself on her sofa, buried her face in her hands, and gave way to a burst of tears.

CHAPTER IX.

OPPOSITION SIDE.

"WELL, Vincent, you have returned to a strange house; strange doings have there been during your absence." Such were the words with which Arabella had greeted her young brother, when, on his first arrival, he had burst into the drawing-room, with all the impatient joy of a boy just emancipated from school.

"You'll hardly believe what has happened," said Lousia.

"Why, what's the matter?" exclaimed Vincent, looking in surprise from the one to the other.

"We none of us can tell where we may find ourselves in another month," continued Louisa. "I foretell that I shall be finishing my education in Jersey, and Arabella in the Isle of Man."

"What has happened?" cried Vincent impatiently; "anything in which our pretty step mother is concerned?"

"*Pretty* step-mother, indeed!" exclaimed Arabella. "She has begun to change and overturn everything in the house. Nothing is free from her meddling. She has turned off Mademoiselle Lafleur without so much as the shadow of a reason."

"Turned off mademoiselle!" cried Vincent. "Well, I don't break my heart about that; but it was a bold stroke for a beginning."

"Then Mrs. Ventner."

"Mrs. Ventner!" echoed Vincent in amazement. "I should have as soon expected to hear of her moving the Monument of London!"

"It won't end here," said Lady Selina oracularly, pursing in her thin lips, as if to restrain them from uttering some dread prognostication.

"Is it really Mrs. Effingham who is turning every-thing topsy-turvy?" cried the schoolboy; "why, she looked as gentle as a dove!"

"A dove!—she's a vulture," said Louisa.

"A vampire!" muttered her sister.

"What I cannot bear," observed Lady Selina, "is the art with which she conceals her designs. Smooth above, false beneath—wearing a mask of such perfect innocence, that she would take in any one who was unaccustomed to the ways of the world. I confess," she added, in a tone of self-depreciation, "that I was deceived myself by her manner."

"Oh! if she's artful, I shall hate her," exclaimed Vincent; "I can't endure anything sly."

"And so hypocritical," chimed in Louisa; "she would pass herself off for such a saint. I believe that poor dear mademoiselle's grand offence was liking a French book that was a little witty—a book which Mrs. Effingham unluckily hit upon when she came spying into our school-room in her fawning, hypocritical manner."

"And to bring in such an ally to support her, before she dared let us know what she had done."

"Yes," said Lady Selina, "I am perfectly convinced—and I am one not often mistaken—that the arrival of Captain Thistlewood was a preconcerted arrangement."

"Captain Thistlewood—who may he be?" inquired Vincent.

"Mrs. Effingham's uncle," replied Louisa. "The funniest old quiz—"

"The most blustering savage—"

"A low, vulgar fellow," joined in Lady Selina; "one who thinks that he may swagger in a gentleman's house as if he were on the deck of a whaler."

"And does papa suffer it?" exclaimed Vincent.

"Mr. Effingham is infatuated, quite infatuated,"

said the lady, apparently addressing the fire and
not any one present, and speaking so low, that
Vincent had to lean forward in order to catch her
accents. "I do not know why it should be—I do
not pretend to guess, but he certainly has not been
like the same man ever since his second marriage."

"Papa has grown much graver," observed Louisa.

"And sadder," joined in Arabella.

Lady Selina only uttered an "Ah!" with a slight
jerk of the head; but what a world of meaning
was condensed into the brief exclamation! Compassion for the infatuated husband, contempt for
the manœuvring wife, sympathy with the persecuted
children. It was the sigh of wisdom and experience
over what was wrong in the world in general, and
in the Effingham family in particular.

It is no wonder that Vincent was not proof
against the contagion of prejudice, hatred, and
malice, when entering the scene where they all were
rife. He threw himself, heart and soul, into the
cause of the insurgents, in the war of independence;
and determined, with all the vehemence of boyhood,
to oppose his step-mother in everything, and not to
be daunted by the "swaggering bully," whom she
had so cunningly brought to London to aid her in
tyrannizing over his sisters, and altering all the good
old customs of the house.

Clemence sat lonely and heavy-hearted in her own room, her eyelids swollen with weeping. She felt so unwilling to face the family at the approaching meal, that twice her hand was on the bell-rope, to summon a servant to convey the message that, having a severe headache, she would not come down to luncheon. The excuse would have been a true one, for her temples throbbed painfully, and a weight seemed to press on her brain ; but a little reflection induced Clemence to change her intention. When a trial is to be faced, the sooner and the more boldly that it is faced the better ; the nettle-leaves grasped by a firm hand are less likely to sting than when touched by a timid and shrinking finger. There would be moral cowardice in secluding herself from envious eyes and bitter tongues, which would only serve to encourage malice. But Clemence's strongest incentive was consideration for her uncle, who might return early, and who must not be left to face the enemy alone ; so she washed all trace of tears from her eyes, and descended at the summons of the gong. Clemence was glad to find that Captain Thistlewood was yet out on his exploring expedition.

Lady Selina did not please to appear at table. Mrs. Effingham breathed more freely in her absence. But the meal was a very uncomfortable one, as must

ever be the case where hatred and strife are guests at
the board.   Hardly a word was spoken *to* Clemence,
but many were spoken *at* her ; every effort which
she made to commence conversation ended in making
her more painfully aware of her position in regard
to her husband's children.   Even her meek and
quiet spirit might have been roused to anger, had
not the recollection of her debt, of the confession of
extravagance to be made to Mr. Effingham, rendered
her too much dissatisfied with herself to be easily
stirred up to indignation against others.

Clemence would willingly have taken an airing
in her carriage during the brief hours of the winter's
afternoon — the rapid motion, the freedom from
vexatious interruptions, would have been welcome
to her harassed mind ; but Lady Selina was certain
to require a drive, and, as usual, it was yielded up
to her by Mrs. Effingham, rather as a matter of
right than of courtesy.   Clemence contented herself
with a rapid, solitary walk in the square.

The air was intensely cold, but its freshness
braced and invigorated her spirits, and helped to
restore them to their wonted healthy tone.   The
dark clouds which flitted across the sky, the leafless
trees whose dark branches waved in the gale, in
their very wintry dreariness spoke to the young
heart of hope.   Those clouds would soon be succeeded

by sunshine. Spring would clothe those bare boughs with beauty, the piercing blast would change to the soft zephyr beneath the genial influence of a milder season! And were not bright days in store for herself! Clemence struggled to throw off her depression, made earnest resolutions, breathed silent prayers, and determined not yet to despair even of conquering hatred by the power of gentleness, and prejudice by the strength of patience.

"There goes one of Fortune's favourites!" remarked Lady Praed to her daughter, as, driving through Belgrave Square, she recognized Mrs. Effingham; "young, lovely, rich, with good health, good establishment, good position—she has everything that the world can give. I should think that Mrs. Effingham must be one of the happiest beings to be found on the face of the earth!"

CHAPTER X.

SOCIAL CONVERSE.

"YOU cannot, dearest, blame my folly, or wonder at my extravagance, more than I do
myself," were the concluding words of Clemence, as, with the timidity of a child
acknowledging a fault, she laid on the
desk before her husband the heavy bill of Madame
La Voye.

Mr. Effingham opened it in silence. If his young
wife had ventured to raise her downcast eyes to his
face, she would have viewed there, not anger, not
sorrow, but a peculiar and unpleasing expression
which flitted across it for a moment, as a bat wheels
suddenly between us and the twilight sky, visible
for a space so brief that we can hardly say that we
have seen it. As it was, Clemence only heard the
words of her husband, as he folded the paper, and
placed it in his desk, "Fifty pounds more or less—
what matters it! you may leave this for me to settle."

Not one syllable of reproach, not even a hint of displeasure! What intense gratitude glowed in the heart of Clemence, deepening, if possible, the fervour of her love for the most noble, the most generous of men! But when she attempted to express something of what, she felt, Mr. Effingham suddenly changed the subject; it appeared to be irksome, almost irritating to him to receive the grateful thanks of his wife.

The evening closed far more joyously to Clemence than the morning had begun. Her husband's presence, as usual, sufficiently protected her from insolence on the part of his family. A pert reply from Vincent to a question asked by his step-mother, drew upon him such a stern reproof from Mr. Effingham, that the boy was for the time effectually silenced. Captain Thistlewood had walked off all his fierce indignation, and finding that the domestic tempest had subsided into an apparent calm, he made no attempt to stir up the sleeping elements of discord, but, on the contrary, exerted himself to spread around him the atmosphere of good-humour in which he himself habitually lived. His flow of conversation was almost incessant. Having on that day ascended to the ball of St. Paul's, and explored the depths of the Thames Tunnel, he was equally primed, as he termed it, for the highest or the deepest subjects.

He had been wandering over a great part of London, from the stately squares of the West End to the crowded thoroughfares of the East; he had seen skating on the Serpentine, horses sliding and struggling up Holborn Hill, and described all with the same minuteness and zest with which he might have portrayed peculiarities in the manners and customs of some island of our antipodes.

"This merry old sailor must be as deceitful as Mrs. Effingham herself," thought Vincent. "If I had not heard that he was a bully and a savage, I should have thought him an uncommonly jolly old chap!"

"I took an omnibus back," said Captain Thistlewood; "for what with the 'getting up stairs' at St. Paul's, and the walking about for hours in the streets, I found myself tolerably well tired. That reminds me," he turned towards Vincent,—"that reminds me of the riddle, 'What is always tired, yet always goes on?' Will you guess it? Bad hand at riddles —eh? It is a *wheel*, to be sure; so that brings me back to my omnibus.

"We were a pretty full party in it, now one dropping in, then another out,—men of business from the city, clerks from the bank; one I noticed with a broad-brimmed hat, another with a smart new tile, cocked roguishly on the side of the head. They

talk " (here he addressed himself to Louisa) " of tell-
ing the character of a man by the bumps on his head :
I think that one might tell something by the style
of his hat ; he has a choice in one thing, and not in
the other. Well, presently the man who stands on the
door-step puts his head into the conveyance. 'Gentlemen and ladies,' says he, 'have a care of your
purses ; there's two of the swell-mob in the 'bus.'
So, as you may imagine, we gen'lmen and ladies
(the ladies consisting of one good fat old dame opposite me, with a well-stuffed bag on her arm, or
rather on her knee) looked awkwardly round on our
companions, half smiling, as if to say, 'Which of us
are the thieves ?' I thought that the fat dame
opposite kept rather a suspicious eye upon me, and
held her hand tight over the opening of her big bag,
afraid that some one should feloniously make off with
her sandwiches or sausages. Presently the man
with the new hat, dashing neck-tie, sparkling pin,
and diamond studs to match, puts his hand into his
pocket : 'I've a large sum about me,' he mutters
half to himself, half as if apologizing to us for de-
priving us of the pleasure of his society, and out he
pops with all convenient speed. Then he in the
broad-brim gives signs of following ; he was at the
very inner end of the omnibus, and had to push past
us all to get out. 'I've a thousand pounds on my

person,' says he, and so gets down, off, and away! I could not help saying to my old lady, 'There are more purses than two the safer for the discretion of these good gentleman : depend on't, we've now nothing more to fear from the two dangerous members of the swell society !' "

" 'Tis conscience that makes cowards of us all," observed Mr. Effingham with a smile.

" It reminds me," said Clemence, "of an Eastern tale of a merchant, who, having been robbed of a large quantity of cotton, and entertaining suspicions of the honesty of several of his acquaintance, invited all whom he doubted to a social meal. In the midst of his entertainment he suddenly exclaimed, with affected indignation, 'Why, what audacious rogues are these, to steal my cotton, and then every one come to my house with a bit of it sticking to his beard !' In a moment several hands were raised, each thief laid hold of his own beard, and the merchant, by this involuntary confession, was enabled to single out those who had robbed him."

" We leave all that sort of work to the detective police," observed Lady Selina.

" Yes, in old England," replied Captain Thistlewood ; " it is a different matter in some other countries that I have heard of, where the constables and the highwaymen form a kind of joint-stock company,—the robbers the active managers, the police the *sleeping partners*—ha! ha! ha! What was the book, Clemence, in which we read that good story of the Englishman in Rome?" The eyes of Vincent brightened at the idea of a story; he unconsciously edged his chair nearer to that of the captain.

"I do not recollect the story," replied Clemence; "let us by all means have it."

"An Englishman was on a visit to the city of Rome, and he had been told that bandits were plentiful there as blackberries, and that a man there thought as little of cutting a throat as he would in France of cutting a caper, or a joke in the Emerald Isle. John Bull had, therefore, been advised by no means to take his constitutionals after the sun had set.

"Our friend, however, once received an invitation to an evening party, which he had a mind to accept; and, thinks he, 'A stout heart and a good crab-tree cudgel will make me a match for any brigand that breathes!' So he went to his party, took a cheerful glass (maybe did not confine himself to one), and then set out in the darkness to return to his lodging in Rome. Now, our Englishman was a bold fellow, but that night he could not help thinking a little of what he had heard of stilettoes, and stabbing, and all that sort of thing. Suddenly a man coming in an opposite direction knocked right up against him, and then hurried on with rapid step. Our friend clapped his hand on his watch-pocket—never a watch was there!"

"The man must have robbed him!" exclaimed Vincent.

"So thought our Englishman, and he was not one to part with his property lightly. Turning round sharp, he rushed after the fellow, overtook him, seized him by the throat, shouted, 'Oriuolo!—watch!' in the best Italian that he could muster, and was well rewarded when a watch was thrust into his hand by the half-throttled, gasping Roman!"

"The robber had caught a Tartar!" exclaimed Vincent.

"The Englishman went home in triumph. He could not help boasting a little of his exploit when he and his family met round the breakfast-table. 'Well, it is odd enough,' said his sister, 'but I could have been sure that I saw your watch hanging up in your room last evening after you had gone to your party.' The Englishman stared for a moment, clapped his hand to his forehead to catch the thought which suddenly darted across it, pulled out from his pocket the watch which he had taken from the Italian—and lo! it was no more his than the clock at the Horse-Guards! He recollected that he had left his own watch at home, as a measure of precaution. So, instead of having been attacked, as he had imagined, by a brigand, he had played the brigand himself, and had actually robbed a poor fellow of his property, under the idea of recovering his own!"

Vincent could not help laughing. "It is the first time," he exclaimed, "that an English gentleman ever acted as a thief!"

"I wish that I could say as much, my boy," observed Captain Thistlewood, slowly sipping his glass of port. "I'm sorry to say that I've met with pickpockets, even in the higher ranks of life, quite as dangerous as the gentlemen of the swell-mob in my omnibus. I've known a man, and one who drove his cabriolet too, go to a shop and order goods to the amount of hundreds of pounds, aware all the time that he had as little chance of paying for them as of discharging the national debt. I've met with another, looked upon as a man of honour, who built up a grand establishment upon the fortunes and credulity of others, who ate his turtle, and drank his claret,— ay, and asked his friends to share in the feast,— knowing all the time that he was spending the money of those who had confided their all to his care. Such men are, in my eyes, pickpockets— heartless pickpockets—for they not only violate honesty, but abuse a trust, and add hypocrisy to theft ! "

" Let us adjourn to the drawing-room," said Mr. Effingham abruptly, pushing back his chair from the table.

CHAPTER XI.

" HEARD there was glorious skating on the Serpentine yesterday!" cried Vincent. "I'll be off there this fine morning, and see the fun!"

"I'll go with you," said Louisa; "I'm sick to death of both books and work. Belgrave Square is as dull as a city of the dead; I want to go where a little life is stirring!"

"Pray, on no account venture on the ice," cried Clemence; "the weather is so much milder to-day, that I feel sure that there must be a thaw."

"I suppose," said Louisa very pertly, "that I may use my own judgment in the matter. I happen to possess a little common sense, and have not the slightest wish to be drowned."

"I am sure that you are greatly indebted to Mrs. Effingham for her tender anxiety on your account," said Lady Selina very ironically, glancing up from the last number of *Punch*.

"That old mischief-maker!" thought Captain Thistlewood; "we should all get on well enough but for her! What a blessing it would be to Clemence if the proud dame could once be got out of the house.—Well, young folk!" he said aloud, "if you want some one to see that you don't make ducks and drakes of yourselves, I'm your man; I'll go to the park with you myself!"

"We don't want your company," said the school-boy rudely; "I can take care of my sister."

"A footman will follow us," added Louisa superciliously; "I may meet friends in the park, and it would cause too great a sensation amongst them if I were to be seen escorted by Captain Thistlewood!" and so saying, with a mock reverence she quitted the room, and was followed by Vincent whistling.

The old sailor did not appear to understand the implied satire, or to be aware that an earl's grand-daughter could possibly be ashamed to be seen with an unfashionable companion. But if his simplicity warded the insult from himself, it glanced off from him to wound the more sensitive spirit of his niece.

"You will escort me, dear uncle," said Clemence; "it will be such a pleasure to walk with you again;"

"Presently, my dear," replied the captain, seating himself on the sofa, of which the greater part was occupied by the stiff silk flounces of Lady Selina.

"I will put on my bonnet—"

"Do not hurry yourself," was the sailor's quiet reply. The truth is, that he had resolved upon having a *tête-à-tête* with Clemence's arch tormentor, and was revolving in his honest mind how best to make it clear to her apprehension, without showing discourtesy to a lady, that as two suns cannot shine in one sphere, no more can two mistresses bear rule in one dwelling. Captain Thistlewood had sufficient observation to perceive that Lady Selina's influence lay at the root of all the bitterness and unkindness which Clemence was called on to endure, and he considered that it would be a master-stroke of diplomacy, could he induce the grand lady voluntarily to resign a position which he could not think that she had any right to hold in the house of his niece.

Lady Selina was also meditating, though her eyes appeared to be rivetted upon *Punch.* She was pondering how Mrs. Effingham's new and strange ally, formidable from the straightforward vehemence of his manner, and his invulnerability to personal insult, could best be coaxed, since he could not be chased from the field. These were strange opponents left to face each other alone,—Simplicity *versus* Art

—the warm-hearted, honest old sailor, *versus* the cold, calculating woman of the world !

Lady Selina was the first to commence the conversation. She laid her paper down upon the cushion beside her, and turning towards her auditor, observed with an air of affected indifference, as if merely fulfilling an office of common courtesy to a guest, "You must greatly miss, Captain Thistlewood, the delightful serenity of the country. I dare say that, after a life spent in charming seclusion, you find London a sad, noisy, bustling place."

" I like it—I like it," replied the old sailor goodhumouredly; "there was never anything of the hermit about me. I was knocked about the world for many a long year, and rather like to live in a bustle, and see plenty of my fellow-creatures about me. No babbling stream pleases my old eyes so much as the stream of people down Oxford Street."

Lady Selina was instantly upon another tack. "I perfectly agree with you," she said; "and I must own " (here she lowered her voice confidentially) " that Belgrave Square is a great deal too dull and out of the way for my taste."

" Is it ? " cried the captain eagerly.

"So far from the best shops, all the exhibitions —from everything, in short, that gives its charm to the great metropolis."

"So it is—the dullest spot in all London," was the hearty rejoinder. "She's really preparing for a removal," thought the exulting captain.

"Now, there are a great many excellent lodgings a great deal nearer to the centre of the city—reasonable, too," pursued Lady Selina, imagining that her fish was approaching the bait, and that, by a little delicate management, she could land him in some convenient spot well removed from the Effingham mansion. "I should say, now, that Bloomsbury Square is a very centrical situation."

"I've no doubt of it—no doubt of it at all !" cried the captain, who had not the faintest idea of the locality, but caught something rural in the sound of the name.

"And you see, Captain Thistlewood," continued Lady Selina, feeling her line with dexterity and caution,—"you see that there is a freedom to be enjoyed in a life of independence, which must necessarily be resigned by any one forming a member of a large establishment. One is not tied down to hours—one can indulge little fancies and tastes without encroaching upon the comfort of others." She paused and glanced at her auditor, to see whether she might venture on a little stronger pull.

The face of the captain was becoming quite

radiant. "You feel and think exactly as I do, ma'am," he exclaimed.

"It must be so painful to a refined mind," pur-sued the lady, "to contemplate the possibility of being a little in the way of causing any inconveni-ence,—any disturbance of arrangements,—any—"

"Any bickerings in the family, you would say," eagerly joined in the captain; "yes, yes, you express my very thoughts. It does not do to have many wills in one house,—one pulling this way, another that. It is far better to meet now and then as good friends, than to live under one roof with per-petual jarring."

"Then, perhaps, you perceive the advisability of soon looking out—"

"Looking out for lodgings?" interrupted the old gentleman. "I'll do so with the greatest pleasure in life! I'm quite at your ladyship's service. I'll hunt half London over, but I will get a place to suit you!"

"To suit *me!*" exclaimed the astonished lady. As the words were upon her lips Clemence re-entered the room, and her uncle, too full of his success to keep it to himself, cried out as he got up to meet her, "Had we not better put off our walk, Clemence? I'm going off at once to look for lodgings for Lady Selina in Bloomsbury Square."

Clemence's blue eyes opened wide in astonishment; she turned them inquiringly towards Lady Selina, who rose from her seat with the dignity of which even surprise and anger could not deprive her. "There are some people," she said bitterly, "who mistake impertinence for wit, and pride themselves on their talent for raising a laugh, even if it be at their own expense. Captain Thistlewood is an adept in the art ; but he may learn that under my brother-in-law's roof such jesting may be carried too far ; " and she swept out of the room without vouchsafing a single word of explanation to the wondering Clemence.

The captain remained perfectly silent until the rustle of the lady's silk was heard no more on the staircase, and then burst into a loud fit of uncontrollable mirth. "A regular Irish blunder ! " he exclaimed, as soon as he could command his voice ; "Politeness and Policy bowing each other so ceremoniously out of the house, that they knocked their heads together at the door ! " and he laughed and chuckled over his own mistake, and that of the astute Lady Selina, long after he and Clemence had quitted Belgrave Square on their way to the scene of the skating.

CHAPTER XII.

A PLUNGE.

THE park presented a gay and animated appearance. Crowds of pedestrians were sauntering to and fro on the shores of the Serpentine to watch the rapid and graceful evolutions of the skaters. Rings of spectators were formed on the ice itself around the most practised proficients; while without these exclusive circles little ragged urchins, some without jackets, some minus hats or caps, amused themselves by gliding along extensive slides—their cheeks glowing with the exercise, their faces looking as full of enjoyment as that of the most aristocratic skater who cut the figure S on the ice.

Clemence and her companion were much amused by the scene, though the lady did not fail to remark in how many spots the warning post, marked "Dangerous," had been inserted, and to notice that the circles of spectators on the Serpentine were beginning to be rapidly thinned, while a very large majority of persons preferred *terra firma* to the ice. The wind had shifted to the west, the air had become sensibly milder, the icicles which had hung from the trees were dripping to the earth like tears, and the round, red sun, glowing like a fiery ball in the sky, was making his influence to be felt.

It was some time before Clemence discovered those for whom her eye was seeking amongst the crowds. She saw them at last on the frozen Serpentine, walking together, their young countenances rosy with the cold. Vincent was laughing and talking to his sister, imitating the awkward movements of some skater whom he had seen making his *debût* on the ice, when he caught the eye of his step-mother, towards whom he happened at the time to be approaching.

"I say, Loo, there's that woman and her tame bear come to hunt after us, as if we could not be safe unless tied to her apron-strings! I vote we turn round sharp and cut them!"

"I think that I see some of my friends at the other side of the Serpentine," said Louisa; "I wish that we could get across to them,—but only— did you not fancy that the ice just now gave a crack!" and she grasped the boy's arm in a little alarm.

"Oh, nonsense!" exclaimed Vincent; "the ice is as hard as a rock!"

A loud, clear halloo came ringing to them across the ice.

"I say, I won't stand that; I am not accustomed to be hallooed to, as if I were a cab-driver on a stand—"

"Or a dog," suggested Louisa: "just look how the vulgar old man is making signs to us to come off the ice."

"He may shout himself hoarse, and flourish away till his arms ache," said Vincent, "we'll stop here as long as we choose.   Just come along this way, Louisa."

Again, as the young Effinghams turned their steps towards the further shore of the Serpentine, again came that loud, warning halloo.   It was not un-heard, but it was unheeded.   Then Louisa stopped short, trembling violently—there was a sudden crash—shriek—splash—and on the spot where Cle-mence had a moment before beheld the two well-known forms on the surface, with horror she could distinguish nothing but a black pool of water, with an ill-defined margin of broken, jagged ice around it!

Her cry of anguish mingled with the short, stifled scream of the miserable Louisa.   Captain Thistlewood uttered no exclamation; before his niece could realize what was passing beside her, he had flung his great-coat at her feet, and, with the instinct of generous humanity, was darting across the ice to the place where the Effinghams had disappeared! He reached it while the air-bubbles were yet floating on the surface of the fatal pool, and plunged in without an instant's hesitation. Clemence's cries for help were bringing speedy assistance, but they seemed to be unconsciously uttered. Almost petrified with terror, she stood on the shore, watching with straining eyes and blanched cheek that dark spot fraught with such fearful interest.

There is a hand grasping the ice!—yes.—no! the brittle substance has broken under the drowning grasp—yet there it is again! and now—oh, thank Heaven! a dripping head emerges!—then another! —a boy, supported by a strong arm, his hair hanging in wet strands over his face, is clinging, scrambling, on to the surface of the ice! Clemence stretches out her arms, and, impelled by an irresistible impulse, springs forward several paces on the frozen Serpentine, but is stayed by the firm grasp of one of the spectators.

"He has dived again!—fine fellow! he is saving the lady!" cried many voices. "Where are the officers of the Humane Society? Ah, here they come! here they come! God speed them!" and, with a rumbling, rushing sound, the machine on skates, invented by ingenious humanity to rescue the drowning from death, is pushed rapidly on to the spot, and plunged into the dark hole on whose brink, in an agony of apprehension, now stands the shivering, gasping, dripping Vincent.

Moments appear hours to Clemence—all power of uttering a sound is gone—the voices around her seem rather as if heard in the confusion of a horrible dream, than as if actually striking upon her waking sense. Oh, that it were but a dream!

"They can't find 'em!—they must have floated under the ice,—got entangled in the weeds!—'twill be too late—too late to save them!" Then suddenly a loud, glad cheer burst from the excited spectators, as a senseless form, with its wet garments clinging closely around it, and long, clotted tresses streaming unconfined by the crushed and dripping bonnet, was lifted triumphantly out of the water.

"She's saved! she's saved!" shouted a hundred voices; "but the brave fellow!—the gallant old man!—they'll never recover him alive!"

Clemence remained as if rooted to the spot, her lips parted, her hands clasped, her soul gushing forth in one inarticulate prayer. Louisa was carried to the society's receiving-house, a large crowd accompanying her to the door; but Clemence was not in the crowd. Vincent, likewise, would not stir from the spot while the officers were redoubling their efforts to find the body of the captain. Wringing his hands, the boy, with passionate entreaties, promises, even tears, sought to stimulate the exertions of any one and every one who could lend a hand to rescue his brave preserver! After a space—a space, alas! how fearfully long—the ice having been broken in various directions, and the drag let down again and again, a heavy body was raised to the surface. There was not the faintest sign of life in it, though the cold hand yet firmly grasped a fragment of a black lace veil, such as Louisa had worn on that fatal morning! Clemence read no hope on the faces of the experienced men who lifted the body on the ice; but in that terrible moment she neither trembled nor wept. Grasping eagerly at the last chance of restoring life to the inanimate frame, struggling to keep down the feeling of despair which was wrestling in her heart, she hastened with the bearers of the body to the receiving-house, which was not far distant. Clemence was met on the way by her own servant, the one who had followed Vincent and his sister to the park.

"Miss Louisa has been brought back to life,

ma'am," said the man eagerly ; but even such good
tidings fell dulled on the ear of Clemence Effingham,
—it seemed as if at that moment she could think of
no one but her uncle.

"Take her and your young master home at once,"
was all that she could say, as she hurried on, absorbed
in anxiety so agonizing that the peril of Louisa was
half forgotten.

The servant touched his hat, and proceeded to
obey ; but nothing would induce Vincent to return
to his home while the fate of his preserver hung in
the balance.   Louisa was conveyed to Belgrave
Square in a cab ; but wet and half frozen as he
was, the boy clung to the side of his step-mother.

"They will restore him !—the warmth will restore him !—he will—oh ! he must ! —he shall recover !" cried Vincent in an agony of grief.

"Every means will be tried," said Clemence
faintly ; "we, Vincent,—we can do nothing now
but pray!"

Every means was indeed tried, every resource of
science was exhausted, but the vital spark had fled,
and all was in vain !   The pulse had entirely ceased
to beat,—not the faintest breath stirred the lungs
—the brave heart was stilled for ever !   The
death of the gallant old sailor had been a fitting
close for a life of active benevolence.   Death had

come to him suddenly, but it had found him not
unprepared ; it had found him in the path of duty;
it had found him pressing onward toward heaven,
with his pilgrim staff in his hand—faith, hope, and
charity in his heart. He was taken away before
the infirmities of age had dulled his senses, bowed
his frame, or chilled the warm affections of his
heart ; and he was taken away in the very act of
risking his life to save that of a fellow-creature ! Is
there nothing enviable in such a departure ?

Dark, heavy clouds had blotted out the sun from
the sky, when Clemence returned with Vincent to
her home, a lifeless corpse in the vehicle beside her.
Her own calmness appeared strange to herself, but
it was the stunning effect of a terrible shock, which
for a while had almost paralyzed feeling. She was
met in the hall by Arabella, who looked pale, and
whose manner betrayed considerable excitement.

"Louisa is very ill,—goes from one faint into
another,—Aunt Selina has sent for Dr. Howard !"

But not one word of sympathy to the bereaved
Clemence—not one word of regret for the brave old
man ! Arabella averted her eyes almost with a
shudder as the body was borne into the house.
Clemence and Vincent saw it reverently placed on
the bed in the room which the captain had occupied
on the preceding night, and then, when the servants

had quitted the apartment, both sank on their knees
beside it and wept.

Clemence's burst of sorrow was violent, but brief;
she folded her step-son in her arms, drew him close
and closer to her heart, and it was like balm to her
bleeding spirit to feel the boy's tears on her neck.

" Oh !" cried Vincent passionately, "if I had not
treated him so ill!—if I had not laughed at him,
mocked him, insulted him !   And he will never
know how sorry I am !   But he did not die saving
me ! no, no,—his life was not lost for me !" the
boy's voice was choked in his sobs.

" My Vincent—it was God's will—we must not
murmur !   We must think on the happiness which
we trust one day to share with him who has gone
before us.   My care must now be for you—*he* is
beyond our aid !   You must have rest, and warmth,
and dry clothes instantly, my Vincent ; your hands
are cold as ice, your very lips colourless and white,
—come with me at once to your own room—your
comfort must be my first thought now."

And then, with the tenderness of a mother, Clemence tended her boy.   She insisted on Vincent's
at once retiring to rest, prepared a warm beverage
to restore circulation to his chilled and shivering
frame, chafed his numbed hands within her own,
and spoke to him soothing words of tenderness and

love. Clemence left him at last dropping into slumber, and then bent her rapid steps towards the apartment of Louisa, about whom she had felt less anxiety, as knowing her to be under the care of her sister and aunt.

Mrs. Effingham met Dr. Howard quitting the room, accompanied by Lady Selina. The countenance of the physician was grave.

" The shock to so delicate a constitution has been very severe," he said in reply to a question from Clemence ; "an increase of fever is to be apprehended. I should certainly recommend that some one should sit up with Miss Effingham during the night."

" I will watch beside her," said Clemence.

CHAPTER XIII.

THE CHAMBER OF SICKNESS.

IERCELY raged the wind through that night; angrily it shook the casements, howled in the chimneys, dashed the winter-shower against the panes! One pale watcher sat listening to the storm beside the couch on which lay stretched a restless, fevered form : Clemence held her vigils in the chamber of sickness. Weary and exhausted though she was, sleep would have fled her eyelids on that night, even had she had no reason for watching. The events of the preceding day had been to Clemence as a terrible vision, and she was thankful for some hours of solitude and comparative stillness in which to collect her thoughts, calm her agitated mind, and cast the burden of her grief at the feet of her Master. The faintest sound from the restless invalid brought Clemence to her side, moving with noiseless step, like a ministering spirit, to bathe the fevered brow, administer the

cooling draught, smooth the pillow of the suffering
Louisa. During the intervals between such gentle
services the step-mother sat quietly at a little table,
where the dim-burning taper threw its faint light
on the leaves of her Bible. Clemence read little—
her mind during that night had scarcely power to
follow any consecutive train of thought; but every
now and then her eye rested on the page, and her soul
drew richer comfort from a single verse, pondered
over, dwelt upon, turned into prayer, than to a careless reader the whole of the sacred volume might
have afforded. Clemence thought much upon her
uncle; and even in these first hours of bereavement
her meditation on him was sweet. For him she
could no longer pray, but she could praise! She
thought on Vincent also—of the warm gush of
generous emotion which had broken through the ice
of reserve. Fondly Clemence thought on the boy,
and every thought linked itself with a fervent peti-
tion for him to the throne of mercy. Nor was the
sufferer beside her forgotten. As Clemence gazed
on the poor girl's pallid face, and heard her restless
moans, no feeling towards her step-daughter remained
but that of tender, sympathizing compassion. The
heart of Clemence was softened by sorrow—quiet,
submissive, holy sorrow; and there seemed to be no
room left in it now for any bitter, resentful emotion.

These were solemn, peaceful hours to Clemence, though a tempest raged without the dwelling, and sickness was within, and in one of the lower apartments lay the lifeless remains of one who had been very dear. The Almighty can give His children "songs in the night;" His presence can brighten even the chamber of sickness, even the couch of death.

The winter's sun was just rising when Arabella softly entered the room ; and as Louisa had at length sunk into a quiet slumber, Clemence resigned for a while her watch over the invalid to her sister. Mrs. Effingham then hastened to her husband to relieve his mind regarding his daughter. She had hardly seen him since the accident, and gladly now sought the comfort of his sympathy and affection. Her next thought was for Vincent. She went to his room—it was empty; to the public apartments—he was not there. She found the boy in the darkened chamber in which lay the captain's remains, gazing earnestly on the features of the dead, as though a lingering hope had yet remained that life might return to them once more. Clemence pressed a fervent kiss upon her step-son's brow, and left her tear upon his cheek.

Clemence felt herself too much exhausted both in body and mind to appear in the breakfast-room that morning; she feared that she could not restrain before her husband emotion that might distress him, and she shrank from meeting the cold, unsympathizing gaze of Lady Selina. Her eyelids were heavy with watching and weeping, and, retiring to her own apartment, Clemence threw herself on her sofa; and her head had scarcely rested on the cushion before she fell into a deep, untroubled slumber, which lasted for several hours.

Vincent hurried over his breakfast, feeling as if every morsel would choke him, and soon left his father and aunt to conclude their cheerless meal together. Arabella was still keeping watch beside her sister.

"Clemence appears much relieved on Louisa's account," remarked Mr. Effingham, after rather a long pause in conversation.

Something approaching towards a smile slightly curled the lip of the lady—slightly, indeed, but sufficiently to fix upon her the attention of her companion.

"Dear Mrs. Effingham is at that happy age when anxieties do not press very heavily upon the mind," said Lady Selina; "at least, it is evident that she apprehended no serious consequences from the accident to Louisa, or she would never have sent her home in a public conveyance, almost sinking from exhaustion and terror, just rescued from a terrible death, with no attendant but a hired menial."

The brow of Mr. Effingham darkened, but he made no reply, and Lady Selina continued in an apologetic manner: " But dear Mrs. Effingham was not aware how much Louisa was suffering from the effects of long immersion in the icy water ; she did not see her before sending her home, so was, of course, less able to judge of her condition.   Mrs. Effingham was so entirely engrossed with regret for her good old uncle that everything else was entirely forgotten ! "

The irritable cough of Mr. Effingham encouraged the lady to proceed, which she did, after sipping a little of her chocolate, with a meditative, melancholy air.

" It is perfectly natural, perfectly right, that a warmer degree of interest should be inspired by an aged relative, no doubt a very estimable, valuable creature, with whom your dear lady had associated for years, than for a connection, however near, known for a time comparatively so brief.   I must not judge of Mrs. Effingham's feelings by my own—I who have watched my dear sister's orphans from their birth, and bear towards them the affection of a mother !   I own that *I* could not have been an hour in the house before visiting the sick-bed of the pre-

cious sufferer ; but then, I know the extreme delicacy of Louisa's constitution.   I have long regarded
her as a fragile flower, one to be reared like a tender
exotic, almost too fair for this world !"   Lady Selina
softly sighed ; Mr. Effingham rose from the table.

Blessed are the peacemakers.   Have we ever
realized how fearful must be the reverse of that
benediction ?   Of whom can they *be called the children* whose delight is in sowing suspicion, awaken-
ing mistrust—they who would rob the innocent of a
treasure dearer than life, the confidence and affection
of those whom they love ?   Lady Selina rejoiced in
the secret hope that she had done something that
morning to loosen Clemence's strong hold on the
affections of her husband ; that she had with some
skill employed paternal love as a lever to shake that
perfect confidence in which lay the young wife's
power.   Lady Selina saw Mr. Effingham depart for
the city, his brow clouded, and his manner abstracted,
with feelings, perhaps, in some degree resembling
those of the Tempter when he had succeeded in
bringing misery into the abode of peace.   She little
considered *whose* work she was doing, whose example
following ; not the slightest shadow of self-reproach
lay on the conscience of the woman of the world.

In the meantime the weary Clemence slept sweetly,
and at length awoke refreshed.   Sorrow, however,

returned with consciousness; and, springing up like one who fears that some duty may have been neglected, Clemence hastened towards the room of Louisa, which was upon the same floor as her own. She was met in the corridor by her maid.

"Oh, ma'am! Miss Louisa is so dreadfully ill! Lady Selina has sent for another doctor besides Dr. Howard."

"Why was I not awakened?" exclaimed Clemence; and as she spoke, a knock at the outer door announced the arrival of one of the medical men.

Louisa was, indeed, alarmingly ill. Lady Selina had had cause for her fear. With a throbbing heart Clemence awaited the decision of the doctors, who, after seeing their patient, remained together in consultation. It was a time when she would naturally have felt her soul drawn towards Lady Selina by a common dread. But an icy barrier appeared to be between the ladies; and the aunt tacitly treated the young step-mother as one who affected an anxiety which she did not feel,— one who was only adding hypocrisy to heartless indifference. Never are we more acutely sensitive to unkindness than when the heart is lacerated by sorrow; and never had Lady Selina inflicted a keener pang than she did in that interval of anxious suspense.

"Miss Effingham is in a very precarious state,"

was the opinion at length given by one of the medical men, addressing himself to Clemence.

"We must be prepared, I fear, for the worst," rejoined Dr. Howard, "though the patient's youth is greatly in her favour."

"Prepared for the worst," faintly repeated Clemence, as the doctors quitted the house. The words brought with painful force before her mind the thought how totally *unprepared* the unhappy girl was for the awful change which might be so near. She who had lived only for pleasure,—she who had put religion aside as a tedious, gloomy thing, profitable only for the sick and the aged,— charity itself, which *thinketh no evil*, could not have regarded her as prepared; and now but a few days or hours might remain of a life hitherto wasted and thrown away,—precious days or hours, if given to God. "Louisa ought to know her danger," said Clemence gravely and thoughtfully to Lady Selina.

"Goodness me!" exclaimed the aunt in indignant surprise, "you would not kill the poor child outright by talking to her about dying! I know well your sentiments towards her, Mrs. Effingham; but this would be carrying them a little too far."

"God guide me!" murmured Clemence, as, turning sadly away, she glided noiselessly into the sickroom.

"She's a heartless hypocrite—a canting bigot," said Lady Selina, when she joined Arabella in the boudoir. "She's going to frighten the little remaining life out of our suffering darling by her terrible warnings and denunciations!"

"I would not let her enter the room," exclaimed Arabella, almost fiercely.

"My love, she's the mistress here—the absolute mistress. Mrs. Effingham takes particular care that we should all be made fully aware of that fact. We have no power to protect your poor sister against her fanatical cruelty, for so I must call it; and the end is to crown the beginning. Little has our Louisa had for which to thank her step-mother—hypocritical smiles, plenty of soft words, but not a single act of real kindness."

"Mrs. Effingham sat up with her all last night," observed Arabella, with perhaps a latent sense of justice.

"A sop to her conscience!" exclaimed Lady Selina indignantly; "a heathen, a savage could have done no less after yesterday's horrible neglect. To send her home dripping and dying—it makes me shudder to think of it. After such treatment of the dear girl, no one on earth would ever persuade me that Mrs. Effingham possesses a heart."

CHAPTER XIV

THE EFFECT OF A WORD.

HY were two doctors sent for? Did they say I am ill, *very* ill?" exclaimed Louisa with feverish excitement, fixing her hollow eyes anxiously upon the face of her step-mother.

"Lady Selina wished to try every means to make you quite well, dear one," replied Clemence quietly, "and thought it best, therefore, to ask the advice of an additional physician."

"And they think that I'll be quite well soon?" The nervous quiver in the poor girl's voice betrayed her own doubt on the subject.

"You must keep very quiet, and not excite yourself, if you wish to be quite well," said Clemence evasively.

"But what did they say? I wish to know." Louisa made a vain effort to raise herself in the bed.

"They said,—Dr. Howard said, that your youth was greatly in your favour."

"But he did not, he did not think me very ill?"

"He thought you ill, dear Louisa"—as Clemence spoke, she gently laid her hand on that of the sufferer; "but—"

"But not dying—not dying!" The agitated tongue could scarcely articulate the words, while the gaze of the glassy eye became yet more distressingly intense.

Clemence felt the moment exceedingly painful. She dared not deceive a soul which was now, perhaps, on the point of being launched into the unfathomable sea; and yet, her dread lest she should by one word hasten the event which she dreaded, almost overcame her courage. "We will pray that your life may be long spared, dear Louisa," was her reply; "all is in the hands of our merciful Lord; He can restore you to health, and make even this trial a blessing."

"I can't pray," said Louisa, gloomily. "I never thought much upon God in my health—I cannot, dare not think of Him now. It is so terrible, so terrible to die!" She grasped Clemence's hand convulsively.

"And yet some have found it sweet to die."

"Ah! yes,—some; the religious—the good."

" *There is none good save one, that is God*,"
whispered Clemence, gently bending over the sufferer.
" If only the righteous had hope in their death,
there would be no human being who could meet it,
as many can and have done, not only with submission, but joy."

" What do you mean ? " said Louisa faintly.

Then Clemence, in few, brief words, spoke of the
sinner's only stay, of pardon offered to penitence,
forgiveness unlimited and free. She scarcely knew
whether Louisa understood her, though her language
was simple as that in which a little child might
have been addressed. It was a comfort, however,
to feel the nervous grasp of the fevered hand relax,
to see the eye lose its excited glare, and, when she
paused, to hear the voice feebly murmur, "Pray for
me ; I can't pray for myself."

" Clemence sank on her knees, and prayed aloud
—prayed from the very depths of her soul. She
addressed the Almighty as the Father of mercies,
the God of all comfort ; she recommended a feeble
lamb to the care of the heavenly Shepherd. Not
by the terrors of the law, but the strong cords
of love, she sought to draw a wandering soul to her
God. Louisa turned her face to the wall, a few
quiet tears dropped on her pillow ; as she listened,
her spirit was calmed, her excitement subsided,—it

was soothing to hear one of the servants of God pleading for her before the throne.

When Clemence arose from her knees, Louisa was perfectly still, thanked her by a gentle pressure of the hand, and, closing her eyes, looked disposed to sleep. Clemence was thankful that the first step was over—that the sick, perhaps dying girl knew her peril, and might, through that knowledge, be led to seek better joys than those which she might now be quitting for ever. Her fever had not increased ; it had appeared to be a solace to have one to whom she could lay open her doubts and fears— one who would intercede for her with her offended Maker. And how immeasurably precious might be the time still left to her who had been brought up in total ignorance, not of the forms, but of the vital power of religion ! Louisa had never thought of herself as a creature responsible to God, as a sinner condemned in his sight, till the veil between her and the invisible world seemed about to be withdrawn by death, and her soul trembled at the prospect of the unknown terrors that might lie beyond that veil.

Clemence was silently revolving in her mind how words of peace and consolation could be spoken without sacrificing truth or lulling conscience to sleep—how this, her first opportunity of speaking to the heart of her step-daughter, might be most wisely and most gently improved, when Vincent, with the thoughtlessness of a child, suddenly opened the door.

"Oh, come, if you wish to see him again!" said the boy in a loud agitated whisper to Clemence; "the men have brought the coffin already!"

There was enough in the intimation itself to touch a painful chord in the bosom of Clemence, regarding her uncle, as she had done, with mingled gratitude and affection; but her thoughts were instantly turned from her own regrets, by alarm at the effect on Louisa of the inconsiderate words which had reached her in her dreamy, half conscious state. Clemence had endeavoured, and not without success, to lead the mind of the poor girl beyond death itself, to the great and merciful Being who has rendered it to His faithful servants only the passage to life eternal. But the sentence, so thoughtlessly uttered by Vincent, and not half understood by the fevered patient, from whom Clemence had kept the captain's death carefully concealed, brought fearfully before her at once all the array of the king of terrors. The hearse, with its nodding plumes, the black pall, the coffin, the shroud—these were the least frightful of the images which flashed through Louisa's burning brain. With a shriek she sprang up in her bed, rolling her eyes in frantic terror, and clinging to Clemence, as if for life, implored her wildly to save her! Vin-

cent, alarmed at the condition in which he beheld his
sister, and unconscious that he himself had been the
cause of it, hurried to call in the assistance of Lady
Selina and Arabella. A messenger was despatched
to Dr. Howard, another to the city to summon Mr.
Effingham—all was excitement and alarm.

Lady Selina went to the room of her unhappy
niece, who was now raving in fearful delirium, but
did not remain in it long. Her nerves, she said,
could not stand such a scene; and she found her
only solace in repeating again and again, "I knew
that it would be so—I warned Mrs. Effingham of
what would ensue; her cruel, fanatical folly has
driven the poor child mad!"

Before Mr. Effingham's arrival, Louisa, exhausted
with her own frantic terrors, had fallen into a state
of insensibility. Her parched hand yet clasped
that of Clemence in a grasp so firm, that the young
step-mother stood by the bed-side for hours, afraid
to stir or change her position, lest by doing so she
should arouse the miserable sufferer to another
paroxysm of delirium.

While Clemence remained in her standing posture,
till she almost fainted with fatigue and the reaction
of her overwrought nerves, Lady Selina, with char-
acteristic tact, availed herself of the vantage-ground
left to her by a rival's absence, to place every occur-

rence before Mr. Effingham in her own peculiar light. As the anxious father restlessly paced the drawing-room, listening for any sound from the apartment above, Lady Selina described to him his child's most distressing symptoms, and gave her own version of their cause. She rather pitied than blamed Mrs. Effingham, gave her conduct no harsher name than that of indiscretion, yet contrived to make it appear such as might have beseemed some familiar of the Inquisition, whose ears were deafened by ruthless bigotry to the cries of his tortured victim.

Mr. Effingham was at length, and for the first time in his life, much irritated against his wife; and when, late in the evening, Clemence, with tears of thankfulness glistening in her eyes, came to tell him that the sufferer breathed more calmly, and that the fever seemed to have abated, he received her with a cold sternness which struck like a dagger into her heart.

"I shall watch by Louisa again to-night," said Clemence, struggling to keep down the emotion which almost choked her utterance.

"You had better leave such watching to the nurse whom Lady Selina has considerately procured," replied her husband with some asperity; "she has experience and judgment, and the arrangement will be better upon every account."

Not one word of tenderness after all that she had

suffered,—not one look of kindness to repay her for
her devoted nursing of his child during that sleepless
night, that miserable day ! A sensation of dizziness
came over Clemence,—a sinking at the heart,—a
sense of overpowering weariness both of body and
mind. She doubted not that she owed her husband's
displeasure to the offices of Lady Selina, but had
neither spirit nor strength to defend herself from
charges which she rather guessed at than understood.
With a slow, languid step, Clemence returned to the
chamber of sickness, to arrange for the night in compliance with the will of her husband ; but she found
such compliance impracticable. Louisa, whose state
varied from fits of wild excitement to nervous depression, could not endure the sight of a stranger,
and with such agonized earnestness implored her
step-mother not to leave her, that Clemence again
spent the night alone with the suffering girl. The
sound of her voice, the touch of her hand, the soft
notes of a low warbled hymn, seemed to have more
power to soothe the invalid than all the medical art.
Louisa, who, in the time of health, had despised and
disliked her step-mother, appeared now to look upon
her as a protecting angel, whose presence could
guard her pillow from the frightful phantoms conjured up by imagination. She could scarcely bear
that Clemence should quit her side for an instant.

CHAPTER XV.

T was a bright Christmas morn. The sound of the sweet church bells ringing for service reached the dull, darkened chamber in which Clemence sat beside her slumbering charge. She had seen Mr. Effingham and Lady Selina, accompanied by Vincent and his sister, set out in the joyous sunlight on their way to the nearest church. It was sadly that Clemence had watched their departure; she had once looked forward to so happy a Christmas, and now trials seemed to shut her out from enjoyment, even as the half-closed shutter and heavy curtain excluded from the room in which she sat the sparkling rays which shone so brightly on all beside! The tongue that had been wont to give cordial greeting on a day like this lay cold and silent in the coffin below—no other season could remind Clemence so forcibly of her blyth, kindly, warm-hearted guardian, as the joyous season

of Christmas. The lively Louisa, once gay as the
butterfly sporting its silken wings in the sunshine,
was stretched beside her on a bed of sickness ; and
though the apprehensions entertained on the sufferer's account were now of a less alarming nature,
her recovery was still precarious. Beneath these
sources of sorrow lay one deeper—so deep that even
to herself Clemence would not acknowledge its existence. Not for a moment would she entertain the
thought that it was possible to find disappointment
where hope had been sweetest ; any doubt of her
husband being indeed the noblest, best of men, she
would have repudiated as treason. But it *was*
possible that he might be disappointed in her ; her
weakness, her extravagance, her inferiority in everything to himself—thus pensively mused the young
wife—might by this time have become apparent to
one whose judgment was quick and discerning. He
was amongst those who would cast no veil over her
failings—those who would make no allowance for her
inexperience—those who might even misrepresent
her motives, and place her actions before him in a
light not only unfavourable but false. Was not his
manner changing towards her—had he not become
silent, reserved, even stern ?

Such reflections were exquisitely painful to Clemence, whose mind was perhaps rendered morbid by

fatigue and want of natural rest. It is when the frame is weary, and the nervous system unhinged, that fancy conjures up phantoms of dangers perhaps altogether unreal, and seems bent on accumulating causes of pain and regret to brood over in silent gloom. It is an unhealthy state of mind—one of the many forms of sickness to which that most delicate and mysterious part of our constitution is subject. Religion alone can offer for such mental malady a cure—religion, which whispers to the burdened spirit, that though *heaviness may endure for a night,* yet *joy cometh in the morning.*

Clemence was trying to raise her thoughts from earthly fears to contemplation of that great event which was upon that day celebrated—to open her soul to the sunshine from heaven, and in its genial warmth forget the shadows that lay on her path, when a gentle sigh breathed beside her told that Louisa had awakened from her sleep, and turning, Clemence saw the invalid, pale indeed, and with traces of suffering on her features, but with a calm expression of countenance, which showed that the fever had departed.

"You are better, my love?" said the step-mother tenderly.

"Much better, only—so weak!" was the feeble reply. "Why are the church bells ringing?"

"It is Christmas-day; and such a bright clear morning! Your father and the rest of our party have gone to church."

"And you—you have stayed to take care of me here! How good you are! I have not deserved it!"

Few words, and faintly uttered; but how sweetly they fell on the heart of Clemence! They resembled one sunny ray which, straight and bright, had forced its way through the opening of the shutters, and striking on a crystal drop which hung from a mantel-piece ornament, not only gave to the opposing glass the brilliancy of the diamond, but itself breaking in the encounter, painted the wall beyond with all the tints of the rainbow.

"Is Captain Thistlewood in church too?" inquired Louisa.

It was well for Clemence that the darkness of the room enabled her to conceal the unbidden tears which rose to her eyes at the question, but to reply to it was at that moment impossible. Louisa, however, scarcely waited for an answer, following the current of her own wandering thoughts.

"I have behaved very ill to him," she murmured; "do you think that he too will forgive me?"

"He never harboured a resentful feeling against you or any one," replied Clemence with an effort.

"I shall see him again?" inquired Louisa.

"I hope—trust—one day," faltered Clemence, her tears fast overflowing, while her lips formed the unuttered words—"one day—in a better world."

"When I am well I will lead a very different life from what I have hitherto done.   I will think much more of religion and duty.   I would not for worlds go again through all the misery of a time like this ! O Mrs. Effingham, if you only knew the horror of that plunge, the icy cold water gurgling over my head, and the thoughts rushing into my mind; and then I fancied that some one caught hold of me to save me, and there was a moment's hope, and then—"

"You must not dwell on these things—indeed you must not!" cried Clemence, who dreaded a return of the fever; but Louisa was not to be silenced.

"I have had such horrible, horrible dreams," she said, passing her thin hand across her eyes.   "I was drowning, but it was in a fiery sea, all burning and glowing around me; and I fancied that you laid hold of me—and that my dress gave way in your hand—and I plunged down—down—"

"Hush, dear one, hush!" said the young step-mother anxiously; "you must not let your mind recall these terrors.   There are such sweet, peaceful, holy subjects to rest upon—an immovable Rock to

cling to, one over which the waters never can break.
I was going to open the Bible; have you strength
to hear a few verses read aloud?"

"I should like it—and then—you will pray,"
murmured Louisa faintly.

There was joy in that gloomy chamber—joy in
the soul of the pale watcher, the joy of hope, and
gratitude, and love! If there be pure happiness on
earth, it is when a mortal is permitted to share the
rejoicings of angels over a wandering sheep found,
an erring soul brought to its God. Clemence had
never thought the words of Holy Writ so beautiful
as she did now, where every verse, as it flowed from
her lips, was turned almost unconsciously into a
supplication for the poor young listener at her side.
She could not have experienced deeper peace even
kneeling in the house of prayer with her husband,
or joining with the congregation in the hymn of
joyful adoration.

On the following morning the remains of Captain
Thistlewood were consigned to the grave, Mr. Effingham and Vincent, at his own request, following the
hearse as mourners. The day had not concluded
ere the sound of the harp, touched by the hand of
Arabella, and accompanied by her powerful voice,
jarred painfully on the ear of the sorrowing Clemence. Disrespect to the memory of the dead, dis-

regard to the feelings of the living, breathed in the lively Italian air sung in a house from whose door the dark funeral had so lately departed.

It was not till now that to Louisa—the doctors having pronounced her entirely out of danger—the fact of the death of Captain Thistlewood was gently broken by Clemence, who then assumed her own mourning garb. Louisa was startled and shocked; the reflection, "If I had been the one summoned instead of him, where, oh, where would my soul have been now?" impressed more forcibly on her mind the solemn lesson taught to her by her own illness.

But would the impression last? Would that light and volatile mind retain the form into which circumstances had moulded it, when these circumstances themselves should be altered? Would the holy resolutions made on a sick-bed stand when brought to the trial by worldly society, vain pleasures, and evil influence? A clergyman, who had laboured for a great number of years, once recorded his melancholy experience, that, out of *two thousand* whom he had known to give signs of repentance when prostrated by sickness, only *two* individuals evidenced by their conduct after recovery that their repentance had been sincere. Let all who would postpone the solemn work till they are

stretched upon a death-bed, ponder well this alarming testimony.   Friends may eagerly mark the cry
for mercy, wrung by fear of approaching judgment,
as evidence that a broken and contrite heart has
been touched by the Spirit of grace; but the Omni-
scient alone can know whether repentance is indeed
unto salvation, or only as the dew that vanisheth,
as the morning cloud that passeth away.

CHAPTER XVI

QUIET CONVERSE.

"THINK that Sunday is the dullest day in the week," exclaimed Vincent, stretching himself with a weary yawn; "and a wet Sunday is the worst of all."

Clemence put down the book which she had been reading, and joined Vincent at the window, where he was drearily watching the raindrops plashing on the brown pavement, making circles in the muddy pools, and coursing each other slowly down the panes. She seated herself beside him, resting her arm on the back of his chair.

"Some people speak of enjoying Sunday," pursued Vincent. "I'm certain it is nothing but talk. I know Aunt Selina said that she did so one day when our clergyman was making a call. I know that what she does on Sunday is to notice the dress of everybody at church, and find fault with the sermon, and talk over all the plans for the week.

I don't see much enjoyment in that." Nor did Clemence; but she thought it better not to express her opinion.

"Do you enjoy Sunday?" asked Vincent, turning round, so that he could look his step-mother in the face.

"Yes; especially Sundays in the country."

"Where's the difference between Sundays in London and Sundays in the country?" asked Vincent.

Here was an opening for pleasant, familiar converse, and Clemence was not slow in availing herself of it. She talked of her school at Stoneby; gave interesting anecdotes of her girls; told of an aged, bed-ridden woman, who loved to receive a call every Sunday afternoon, always expecting that her visitor would repeat to her the leading points in the morning's sermon. Greatly had Clemence missed her accustomed Sabbath labours of love, her husband having decidedly objected to her undertaking any such in the great metropolis. It was sweet to her now to recall them; and in Vincent, who was thoroughly weary of his own society, she found a willing listener.

"I can fancy that it must be pleasant going to the cottages, where every one is glad to see you," said the boy; "but then there are the long, tiresome

evenings, especially during the winter; how did you
manage to get over them?"

"I sang hymns, and read a good deal."

"Oh, but Sunday books are so dull."

"Do you think so? I find some so interesting."

"I never saw one yet which did not set me
yawning before I had got through half a page."

Clemence went to the book-case without replying,
and returning with a volume of the "History of
the Reformation," resumed her seat by Vincent.
"Would you like to hear a story?" she said, after
turning to an interesting passage in the life of
Luther.

"A story, yes; but I don't want a sermon."

Clemence read with animation and expression,
and Vincent speedily became interested. The history naturally led to questions from the intelligent
boy, which his step-mother readily answered. He
was unconsciously drinking in information upon one
of the most important of subjects.

"How odd it is," exclaimed Vincent suddenly,
"that I should ever have taken you for a Papist!"

"A Papist!" repeated Clemence in a little surprise.

"Why, Aunt Selina told us that your grandmother was a Frenchwoman."

"And so she was, but not a Romanist."

Vincent's countenance fell.   "So you're partly
French, after all," cried he ; " I'm sorry for that, for
I hate the French."

"Should   we   hate   anything   but   sin ? "   said
Clemence softly.

"I'm a regular John Bull ! " cried Vincent, " and
I don't care if all the world knew it !   Britannia
for ever, say I ! "

" You cannot love old England better than I do,"
said Clemence; " but patriotism is one thing, and
prejudice another."

" What do you call prejudice ? " asked Vincent.

" The   determination   to   dislike   some   one   or
something before judgment has had time to decide
whether it merit your dislike or not.   Surely this
is neither reasonable nor right ! "

" I think that we were prejudiced against you,"
said Vincent thoughtfully—" that is, before we knew
you, and perhaps some of us after we had known
you.   We did not wish to like you ; only, you see,
we really could not help ourselves," and the boy
looked up archly into the blue eyes that met his
gaze so kindly.

" Prejudice," observed Clemence, " prevents our
seeing objects as they actually are."

" I see, I see," said Vincent quickly; " prejudices
are like the knots in the glass of one of our windows

at school. They alter the shape of everything that we choose to look at through them; they make straight things crooked, and nothing distinct—even your face would look quite ugly only seen through that glass."

"One would not wish to have one's mind full of such knots," said Clemence, smiling at the school-boy's simile.

"I think that *your* glass is all rosy-coloured!" cried Vincent, "and that makes you look at every one kindly. But Aunt Selina don't deserve it of you. Do you know what she said of you once?"

"I have no wish to hear it, dear Vincent."

"Something about idolatry, which was not at all true; and she said—I did not believe a word of it! —that there is a natural leaning in our hearts toward idolatry. That was downright nonsense, I know. Nobody has idols in England."

"I wish that I could think so," replied Clemence.

"What! do you believe that there are any in this country?"

"I fear that there is scarcely a house in it that is really without one. Idols, dear Vincent, are not merely lifeless figures of silver or gold, such as the poor heathen worship; anything, everything that takes the place of God in the heart,—anything, everything that is loved more than Him is an idol, and brings on us the sin of idolatry."

Vincent sat for a space very silent, revolving his step-mother's words in his mind, then said, "If that be the case, I think that there are idols in this very house. Bella's idol is Pride, Louisa's is Pleasure, Aunt Selina's—"

"Hush !" said Clemence gravely, laying her hand on the arm of Vincent ; "it is worse than useless to find out the idols of our neighbours; our duty is to search for our own. The same volume in which we read, *Judge yourselves, brethren*, also bids us, in respect to others, *Judge not, that ye be not judged*."

"I don't think that I have any idol," said Vincent. after another pause for reflection. Clemence Effingham remained silent.

"Do you think that I have ? " said the boy.

"Are you willing to know, dear Vincent, or will you be vexed if I tell you the truth ? "

"I wish to know it," replied Vincent.

"Then it appears to me, dear boy, as though you had hitherto made an idol of Self-will. It appears to me that when any duty presents itself, 'What do I like to do?' not 'What ought I to do?' is usually your first consideration. You are ready for any kind, generous, noble act, if it accord with your own inclination; but if it run counter to that, duty is sacrificed at once. Is not this putting Self-will in the place of the law of God? is not this bowing to an idol that usurps the authority of God?"

"I never had it put to me in that way before," replied Vincent. "I suppose that it was thinking of what *I liked*, instead of *what I ought to do*, that made me disobey you by going on the ice, and cost that noble old captain——but I do not like to speak of that," said Vincent, interrupting himself, "and it makes you look so sad. I wonder," he cried in an altered tone, "if you have an idol too, and if you try hard to put it away?"

Before Clemence had time to reply to the bright-eyed boy, the door opened, and Mr. Effingham entered. If the heart of Clemence enshrined an idol—if there were one being whose love was almost more precious to her than celestial hopes, whose approbation was almost more fondly sought for than that of her Lord, that idol was before her now!

CHAPTER XVII

GATHERING CLOUDS.

AY by day Louisa regained her strength, and day by day old tastes and impressions revived, and she more eagerly anticipated the time when she should be able to plunge again into a vortex of light amusements. She was still, indeed, courteous, almost affectionate to Clemence, retaining a grateful sense of the kindness which had so tenderly nursed her through a distressing illness. A pretty token of remembrance was received by her step-mother on the anniversary of Clemence's birth-day, accompanied by a few lines expressive of grateful regard. But Lady Selina was gradually resuming her influence over the convalescent; and Arabella was her constant companion. The secession of Louisa to "the enemy's side" was an event not to be suffered by either. Arabella spoke bitterly against Clemence in the presence of her sister, not altogether sparing even the memory

of Captain Thistlewood ; but this had no effect beyond that of annoying Louisa. Lady Selina worked
more cautiously and surely. Gradually she commenced raising anew the wall of prejudice, which
had been swept away as by a flood from the mind
of her niece. She did not deny Clemence's merit,
but she depreciated it—praised her kindness, but
cast suspicion on its motives ; and by many a covert
allusion to " Mrs. Effingham's extraordinary conduct
on the day of the accident," tried to convert the
gratitude of Louisa into a totally opposite feeling.

The world, from which the young girl had for a
time been separated by her illness, like a magnet
possessed more and more attraction the nearer she
approached to it again. The Bible, though not entirely neglected, was often laid aside for the novel ;
and gossip about the fashions, a new dress, or a new
acquaintance, was readily welcomed by Louisa as a
substitute for serious thought. Her conscience was
no longer dead, but its voice was drowned in other
sounds ; the terrors which had oppressed her were
melting away like a dark, dissolving view, into new
bright tints; and when the sick-room was exchanged
for the drawing-room, Louisa seemed to have left
behind her most of the serious resolves and solemn
impressions which had owed their birth only to
fear.

Not contented with her insidious endeavours to
alienate from Clemence the affection which she had
won, Lady Selina employed all her art in throwing
difficulties in the way of replacing Mademoiselle
Lafleur. Her own education, though not more solid,
had been conducted on more fashionable principles
than that of Mrs. Effingham ; and Lady Selina had
little difficulty in making it appear even to her
brother-in-law that she was far better qualified than
the youthful step-mother to choose an instructress
for his children. If Clemence deemed that she had
met with a lady whose high character, experience,
and knowledge were likely to render her services
valuable, Lady Selina at once detected some defect
of manner, education, or age, which would render
it perfectly out of the question to receive her as
governess in Belgrave Square.   The earl's daughter
appeared, by Mr. Effingham's tacit consent, to reserve
to herself a power of negativing every proposition
which did not please her ; and it was evident to
Clemence that this power would never lie dormant
in her hands. The young wife, too timid to court
opposition, too diffident to maintain her own opinion
boldly, except in cases where conscience was concerned, gave great advantage to an adversary well
versed in the tactics of the world, and by no means
scrupulous in making use of its weapons.

The small property of Captain Thistlewood, amounting, clear of needful expenses, to less than a hundred
pounds per annum, had by his death reverted to his
niece ; but the money would not for some months be
available, and in the meantime Clemence, the wife of
the opulent banker, was annoyed by petty pecuniary
embarrassments. Her expenses had been regulated
with the strictest economy since her first and only
visit to Madame La Voye ; but necessary expenditure on mourning, however simple, had involved her
again in difficulties, which harassed without seriously
distressing. Clemence shrank with invincible re-
luctance from applying for money to her husband,
who had so recently generously taken upon himself
the debt which she had so thoughtlessly incurred.
Nor could Clemence conscientiously apply to her
own private use even a fraction of the large sums
appropriated to household expenses; she looked upon
herself as her husband's steward, and scrupulously
acted as such. It thus happened that, in the midst
of luxury and plenty, the young mistress of that
superb mansion found her purse drained of its last
shilling. The consequences of her excessive liberality
and thoughtless expenditure on first coming to London clung to her still ; and it did not lessen her
chagrin to suspect that Lady Selina was aware of
her little difficulties, and secretly rejoiced in the

embarrassments into which she herself had helped
to lead an inexperienced girl.

One afternoon towards the end of January, Mr.
Marsden, the clergyman of the parish, paid a visit
in Belgrave Square. He was a man who laboured
faithfully in his vocation ; and though his manner
might be ridiculed, and his sermons criticised, his
character always commanded respect. Lady Selina
usually brought out for his benefit her most choice
religious phrases. When he feelingly congratulated
the pale Louisa on her deliverance from danger and
her recovery from illness, her aunt chimed in with
such admirable observations on the uncertainty of
life and the necessity for constant readiness for death,
as raised the lady in the eyes of the clergyman. He
was proportionately disappointed to mark Clemence's
apparent coldness on the subject ; for her truthful
nature could not show approval of sentiments, however true, which she knew to be uttered by the lip
of hypocrisy.

The object of Mr. Marsden's visit was to lay before his rich parishioners the pressing necessities of
his poor. The winter was a very severe one. Behind the magnificent mansions of the aristocracy,
want pined and sickness languished. He had come
from the garret of the widow, the loathsome crowded
dwellings of the indigent ; he pleaded the cause of

the orphan, and of those who had no certain shelter from the piercing cold, even in a season so inclement.

Lady Selina shook her head mournfully at the clergyman's description of prevailing poverty, sighed, drew forth her purse, and taking from it the smallest gold coin of the realm, gave it with some excellent comments on the privilege of assisting the poor, and the necessity of supporting all the numerous valuable institutions springing up on all sides for their relief!

Mr. Marsden bowed, and turned towards Mrs. Effingham. Clemence's sympathy for her suffering brethren had been strongly called forth by his appeal; but what could she do to prove it? The mistress of that stately mansion, in her own luxurious apartment, could plead no disability to give. Young Vincent's eyes were fastened upon her; Clemence knew that he expected that the liberality of one who had often spoken to him of the poor, and of the duties of the rich in regard to them, should be in accordance with her principles. There was a short, awkward pause, and Clemence was about to promise to lay the appeal before Mr. Effingham, when Lady Selina drew forth a bank-note from the porte-monnaie which she still held in her hand.

"If your purse is not here, Mrs. Effingham, I shall be most happy to accommodate you," she said with a smile ; and there being no time for reflection, the note was hesitatingly received by Clemence, and transferred to the clergyman, who shortly afterwards quitted the house, leaving the young wife the consciousness of having performed not a liberal, but a foolish act—of being, not the benefactress of the poor, but a plaything in the hands of Lady Selina.

"Shall I never acquire the power of saying 'No,' and lose my childish fear of offending or disappointing?" thought Clemence, greatly discontented with herself. "I am actually in debt to Lady Selina ; but I will not be so beyond this evening. I will speak to my husband frankly, and ask him to advance me some of the interest that will be due to me in June. I will try to be much more prudent and watchful over my expenditure in future, divide my several items of expense, and appropriate a fixed sum to each, so that vanity may never encroach on benevolence, or thoughtless folly leave me again without the means of assisting the poor. I see that economy is not required alone by those whose means are narrow ; true is the saying, that every man, whatever be his wealth, is poor, if he spend a shilling more than he possesses!"

More impatiently than usual Clemence on this evening awaited her husband's return from the city. That return was delayed far beyond the usual hour.

ILL NEWS.

Page 171

Clemence felt, however, at first no uneasiness at his absence. He had had some unusual press of business, or had been delayed by seeing some friend. Twilight deepened into night, the shutters were closed, the lamp was lighted on the table, and many observations were exchanged as to the cause of Mr. Effingham's lateness.

"Papa's watch must have gone backwards," observed Louisa, who, wrapped up in shawl and fur cloak, occupied an invalid's place on the sofa.

"If he were as hungry as I am," cried Vincent, "he'd have no need of a watch! Well, there's no use in watching and waiting; who'll have a game of draughts with me to while away the time?"

"Not I," said Louisa wearily; "there is no use in commencing anything which we may have to leave off in a minute."

"Draughts is the most tiresome game in the world, and only fit for children," added Arabella.

"Set the pieces, Vincent, and I'll try if I cannot beat you," said Clemence, putting aside her work. Vincent readily obeyed, and a game was commenced. Lady Selina took out her watch.

"Really I am becoming uneasy," she said, resolved that Clemence at least should be so. "Mr. Effingham is always so punctual; I trust that nothing serious is the matter!"

"How ill papa has been looking lately," observed Arabella.

Vincent found that his partner was paying very little attention to her game.

"This is the third time that you have been huffed!" he exclaimed; "if you do not take care I shall carry off every one of your men!"

"Mr. Effingham is very much changed; I am distressed to perceive it," pursued Lady Selina. "Six months ago he was the youngest man of his age that ever I saw,—you might have really taken him for thirty,—and now!"

"I was noticing yesterday a streak of grey in his hair," observed Arabella, glancing maliciously towards Mrs. Effingham.

"Wont you move?" cried Vincent rather impatiently to his abstracted partner. Clemence mechanically placed her piece.

"I dare say that papa is worried by business," said Lousia, resuming the thread of the conversation.

"There's a carriage at last!" exclaimed Vincent; but the quick, listening ear of Clemence had caught the sound before he could hear it, and hastily rising, she quitted the room.

"The game's up!" cried Vincent, making a clean sweep of the board, and tossing black and white promiscuously into the box ; "it's a shame, for I had much the best of it."

"Papa must have been taking a long drive," observed Louisa.

"One can judge of that in a minute by the horses," cried Vincent, sauntering up to a window, and opening a leaf of the shutters that he might look out into the night. " Why, that's not our carriage at all, it has only one horse ; I know whose it is, it's Mr. Mark's,—papa's man of business ; what on earth brings him here at this hour ? "

" That's not papa's voice in the hall," said Arabella.

"I fear that something is indeed the matter !" exclaimed Louisa, starting from her seat.

Her suspicion was soon confirmed by the sound of the study-bell violently rung ; then they heard the door open, and Mr. Mark's voice below, calling for water for Mrs. Effingham.

"Something terrible has happened," cried Lady Selina, and the next moment the drawing-room was vacated by all.

CHAPTER XVIII

CALCULATIONS.

"BANKRUPT! stopped payment!" exclaimed Lady Selina, as Mr. Mark repeated to her the substance of the tidings, which, like a sudden blow, had prostrated the spirit of Clemence. The lady and the man of business were conversing alone, Clemence having been removed to her room in a fainting state, attended by Louisa and Vincent.

"Is there no hope—no means of rallying—of struggling through the difficulty?" continued Lady Selina.

Mr. Mark looked very grave, and shook his head.

"I fear that this has been no thing of yesterday. The firm must have been for some time in a tottering state, though appearances were so carefully kept up that the crash took every one by surprise."

"The strangest thing of all," said Lady Selina, "is, that Mr. Effingham himself should, as you tell

me, have disappeared—not have ventured to face
his creditors !"

"It is strange," observed the lawyer almost sternly;
for he was an honest, straightforward man, who had
not learned to regard all things as fair in the way
of business. "It is strange!" he repeated more
slowly : "when the affairs of the firm are wound
up, we shall be better able to account for such a
step on his part. It was this disappearance which
touched Mrs. Effingham so nearly ; she bore the
news of the failure with a degree of firmness which,
I own, surprised me ; but when I informed her that
her husband had fled, she was struck down at once ;
I was seriously alarmed for the consequences."

"Oh ! she is subject to hysterical fits ; they do
not alarm those who know her," said the lady,
whose malice would glance forth even at a time like
this. "Of course Mrs. Effingham must feel the
change in her fortunes ; none shrink from poverty
more than those who have once experienced its
trials."

"Mrs. Effingham is secured from anything approaching to poverty," said the lawyer ; "ample
provision has been made for her comfort. Sixty
thousand pounds were settled upon her not long
after her marriage."

"Sixty thousand pounds ! and settled upon Mrs.

Effingham!" exclaimed Lady Selina; "and what becomes of the rest of the family?"

"As you are aware, madam, the dowry of the late Lady Arabella Effingham, amounting to ten thousand pounds, was, by her will, divided share and share alike between her two surviving daughters. That is safe—invested in Government securities; for the rest, everything—house, furniture, estate—will, doubtless, be seized and disposed of for the benefit of the creditors."

"But the sixty thousand pounds that you mentioned?"

"That sum is settled on Mrs. Effingham; no one will be able to deprive her of that." Mr. Mark's manner was cold and dry, and he soon afterwards closed the interview, leaving Lady Selina in a state of no small excitement and perplexity.

"Clever man of the world, Mr. Effingham," she said to herself, as soon as she found herself alone; "I should hardly have given him credit for the tact to save such a sum out of the wreck. And all settled upon Mrs. Effingham!"—she bit her lip with vexation. "I wish that it had been disposed of in any other manner. Sixty thousand pounds! The interest of that will be—let me see—enough to keep a good house, a carriage. It is much more than she had ever a right to expect. We must not part company, after all. The weak little creature will never be able to manage by herself; and it will suit my convenience better for the family to keep together. Yes," soliloquized the earl's daughter, resting her chin on her hand in an attitude of thought, "it would be folly under these circumstances to part. I must change my tactics a little. I must make her feel me necessary; there must be no division. If I had ever had a suspicion of the turn which affairs would take, I would have played my cards very differently with Clemence Effingham."

Regard for self-interest was striving against prejudice and pride, and, as often happens in hostilities of a more extended nature, the war was ended by a compromise, or rather a treaty of alliance. In a few minutes Lady Selina was gently tapping at Mrs. Effingham's door.

Clemence appeared seated at her little writing-table, pale but tearless. Louisa was weeping beside her. Vincent, standing a little apart, was repeating to himself half aloud, "Poverty is no disgrace," as one who is determined to face the enemy with resolution. It is possible, however, that poverty presented itself to the mind of the boy as little beyond exemption from going to school, and was, therefore, no great trial of his youthful philosophy. Lady

Selina motioned to Louisa and her brother to quit the room, and then seating herself on the sofa close to Clemence, with strange, unwonted show of tenderness, laid her hand on that of the young wife, which lay cold and impassive on the cushion beside her.

"Dear Mrs. Effingham, we are truly partners in sorrow ; for, believe me, my share in this trial is no light one," and the lady heaved a deep sigh.

Clemence remained silent. That Lady Selina grieved for her she could not for a moment believe ; but it was possible that even that cold, worldly heart might cherish a regard for her husband. How could it indeed be otherwise, after such long, intimate acquaintance with one who possessed such power to attract to himself the affections of all who knew him ? Such a thought was quite sufficient to prevent the gentle wife from repelling the sympathy, such as it might be, even of her who had hitherto acted the part of an enemy. It would, however, have been hypocrisy to have accepted it with any warmth of gratitude. The pressure of Lady Selina's thin fingers was not returned, and the eyes of Clemence remained bent upon the floor.

"But, dear Mrs. Effingham," resumed Lady Selina, "this trial has alleviations—great alleviations."

In an instant the blue eyes were rivetted on the countenance of the speaker with an expression of hope. "Alleviations! Then you know where he is,—you have tidings—"

"None, none," replied the lady sadly; "but is it not a comfort to think that your beloved husband, even under the heavy pressure of adversity, thought and cared for his family with a foresight which does him such honour? Mr. Mark, of course, informed you that the sixty thousand pounds settled upon you by Mr. Effingham are safe; the creditors cannot lay a finger upon them."

Lady Selina watched the effect of her words. A bright flush suffused the countenance of Clemence, rising even to her temples, and then suddenly retreating, left it even more pallid than before.

"I did not hear about money—could not think about money," she replied hoarsely, withdrawing her hand from Lady Selina's.

"Your delicacy of feeling, your disregard of worldly considerations is noble—is quite in character," said that lady, with a little touch of sarcasm in her tone; "nevertheless, it must be a great relief to your mind to find that everything is not lost—that, though on a smaller scale, you can still maintain a suitable establishment, still offer a home to those who have dwelt together under this roof."

Clemence pressed her aching brow with both her hands. "Lady Selina, I cannot think, I cannot realize what has happened, far less form plans for an uncertain future. I must hear from my husband, I must learn our actual position, know the full extent of the ruin which has come upon our house. Of one thing I am certain—*certain*," she repeated more earnestly, rising from the sofa as she spoke, "my husband would be the last man to claim or to desire an exemption from the sufferings which may, I fear, fall upon some of his creditors. I feel assured that, when he settled a fortune upon his wife, it was in perfect ignorance of the crash which was so near. Unforeseen events have brought on a crisis, and he will meet it, like himself, with firm courage, unblemished honour, and a conscience free from reproach."

"She is a greater fool than I thought her," was Lady Selina's mental reflection, as she relieved Clemence from her unwelcome presence.

Clemence, notwithstanding her fearless declaration, felt strangely uneasy and anxious. Vincent's childish words recurred again and again to her mind, "Poverty is no disgrace." Why should such words give her pain? She feared to question her own heart as to the reason. Clemence wrote a long letter to her friend Mr. Gray, the faithful counsellor of her youth, detailing to him what had occurred, as far as her own knowledge extended, mentioning to him the words of Lady Selina, and asking him, in the absence of her best and dearest guide, to say whether he thought that she could conscientiously avail herself of resources so considerately provided for her before the day of adversity had arrived. Clemence touched tenderly on the subject. Doing so, even in the gentlest manner, pained her like pressure upon a wound. She shrank from writing a word which, even in the most remote way, could convey the slightest imputation upon the conduct of her husband.

The wings of Time sometimes appear to be clogged with lead. How wearily move the hours when anxious sorrow watches the shadow on the dial! Clemence's prevailing feeling was an intense desire for tidings from her absent lord. If uneasy doubts would arise in her mind, a letter, she felt assured, would remove them. Her husband would make all clear. Whatever had occurred, no fault could rest with him; her loving faith in him was unshaken. Clemence started at every post-knock, and trembled when her room was hastily entered, so nervously was her mind on the watch for tidings.

Louisa was in a state of great depression. The first breath of misfortune was sufficient to lay low the fragile reed, which had no firm support to counterbalance its own weakness. Perhaps there was a secret painful impression on the young girl's

mind that, since God's first visitation had failed to
produce lasting effects, one yet more terrible might
be coming upon her.   Louisa refused to listen to
words of comfort or hope, persisted in viewing everything in the darkest light, and by her tears, com-
plaints, and forebodings, irritated the prouder and
firmer spirit of her sister, which was struggling to
tread misfortunes under foot, and rise triumphant
above them.

On the following day, which was Sunday, neither
Lady Selina nor her nieces quitted their dwelling.
Those who had attended divine service only *to be seen
of men*, naturally absented themselves from the house
of prayer when observation would be painful.   But
to Clemence, weary and heavy-laden, social worship
was a privilege not to be lightly foregone.   In the
solemn exercises of prayer and praise, she trusted to
be raised for a while above the cares and the grief
that oppressed her; the jarred and strained chords
of her heart could yet be tuned to swell the church's
hymn of thanksgiving.   Avoiding mixing with the
stream of the congregation of which she had been
lately a member, Clemence, accompanied only by
Vincent, attended a more distant church.

The preacher's sermon appeared as if addressed
expressly to herself, so closely did Clemence apply
it.   He spoke of the blessedness of that home which

sin and sorrow never can enter, and of the boundless riches of God's grace, so unlike to the treasures of earth which take to themselves wings and flee away. He dwelt on the glories of the heavenly city, till clouds of present affliction seemed to reflect its distant brightness. He then described the heaven in the heart, which may be experienced by the believer while yet a sojourner in a world of trial, yea, even when plunged into the seven-fold heated furnace of *great tribulation*,—the consciousness of the presence of an Almighty Friend, of the support of the everlasting arm, of the possession of that unspeakable love which passeth knowledge, and *is stronger than death!* Tears, but not tears of grief, flowed from the eyes of Clemence as she listened, and her heart seemed able to echo the words of the poet, with which the preacher concluded his address—

> " Give what Thou canst, without Thee we are poor—
> And with Thee rich, take what Thou wilt away."

CHAPTER XIX.

SACRIFICE.

ONDAY came, and with it a letter from Mr. Effingham, bearing the Dover postmark. How eagerly was it received and torn open! The note was a very brief one, and communicated but a vague idea of the position or feelings of its writer. He was on the point of crossing over to France,—hoped that his stay there might be a brief one,—that necessary forms having been complied with, he might soon be able to return to her who was ever in his thoughts. He trusted that her health had not suffered from the shock of receiving tidings which he had not had the courage to communicate to her himself; and he desired his wife, in the conduct of her affairs, to place implicit confidence in Mr. Mark, and to be guided by the judgment of a man of such experience and worth. This was all,—not even an address given ; but such as it was, the letter was a

great relief to Clemence. Her mind had formed
dark forebodings; she had dreaded that sudden illness might have been the result of Mr. Effingham's
distress of mind, and the cause of his not coming
forward personally to meet those whose interests
had been confided to his care. She now felt able
to enter his study again, that little room consecrated
by so many dear recollections, to gather up and
arrange any stray papers that might have been left
there, that her husband, on his return to England,
might find that nothing was missing.

How little that room was altered! The fire
blazing brightly as ever, the familiar tomes ranged
in their accustomed places, the morning's *Times* laid
on the table, the book beside the desk with half its
leaves yet uncut, and the paper-knife marking the
place where Mr. Effingham had lately been reading!
Clemence tried by an effort of imagination to blot
out all remembrance of the last few days, to look
upon what had passed as a dream, and to listen for
that well-known step which would never be heard on
that threshold again! She would not occupy the
arm-chair which she had seen so often filled by her
husband. One thing was changed—but one; the
clock on the mantel-piece, which Mr. Effingham had
suffered no one to touch but himself, which had be-
longed to his father before him, that clock which he

had regularly wound on each Saturday night, stood
silent, with motionless pendulum,—an emblem of the
fortunes of the house.

Vincent followed his step-mother to the study.
The boy was restless and sought companionship, but
Louisa was too melancholy, and Arabella too irritable
to make their society congenial to their brother.
Clemence would at that time have greatly preferred
being left alone with her own sad musings, but she
would not, even by a hint to that effect, drive from
her side the only being who clung to her in her sorrow.   Vincent was therefore allowed to sit beside
her, endeavouring to glean amusement from the
Times, while she slowly and sadly pursued her occupation of collecting scattered papers.   One struck
her eye—its appearance seemed familiar to her ;
upon examination it proved to be the bill of Madame
La Voye—that bill which had cost her such painful
self-reproach.   It had surely been paid long ago ;—
no ! unreceipted, it lay amongst others !   Clemence
bit her lip, but at the moment was startled by a
vehement exclamation from Vincent.

"What a shame ! how dare they write so of
papa !"

Clemence caught the paper from his hand.   Vincent pointed to one of the leading paragraphs ; it
commenced thus:—

" We have again to record a great crash in the commercial world, attended with circumstances which force upon our attention the fact that the laws of bankruptcy, as at present constituted, are inadequate to protect the property of the subject."

Clemence read on, every sentence falling like a drop of glowing metal on her heart; she saw the name most dear to her coupled with duplicity, craft, dishonour!

" We hear on undoubted authority," said the *Times,* " that Mr. Effingham has settled a large fortune upon his wife, with whom the *bankrupt* doubtless looks forward to enjoying in luxurious retirement the spoils of the widow and the orphan. These evasions of law and equity have been of late of such frequent occurrence, that we have learned complacently to behold the giant offender rolling in his carriage, while the meaner felon is consigned to a jail."

The paper dropped from the hand of the miserable wife. Vincent sprang to her side. " It is not true!" he exclaimed passionately; "it is all nonsense and lies!—it is!—oh, say that it is!"

"Leave me, Vincent! leave me!" gasped Clemence; with an imploring gesture she motioned to the door, and, as soon as her command had been obeyed, threw herself down upon the floor and writhed, as if in convulsions of bodily pain! What physical torture could have equalled the agony of that hour! The anguish caused to a loving and conscientious spirit by the errors of the being most beloved, resembles in nature, and is scarcely exceeded in intensity by that of remorse! To Clemence, her husband's

disgrace was her disgrace ; his transgressions seemed
even as her own. So closely was she joined to him
in heart, that the consciousness of personal blame-
lessness brought her no comfort—the shadow which
had fallen on him enveloped her also in its blackness !

"What am I called upon to endure!" was a
thought ere long superseded by another: " What am
I called upon to do?" A gulf of misery was yawning
before the bankrupt's wife—could no personal sacrifice close it ? Clemence started to her feet, took the
writing materials which lay on the table, and hastily
penned to Mr. Mark a scarcely legible note, praying
him to come to her as soon as was possible, as she
needed his assistance and advice. This done, and
the letter despatched, Clemence could breathe a little
more freely. She declined seeing any one until after
his arrival, and as that was delayed for several hours,
the unhappy wife had time to become more calm,
and to revolve in her mind what course of duty lay
before her. Yet the sound of the long waited-for
knock at the door which announced the man of
business, was to her much as that of the hammer-
stroke on a scaffold might be to one doomed to suffer
thereon.

Mr. Mark entered with apologies for delay, of
which Clemence understood not one word. With

tremulous hand she pointed to the *Times*, and could scarcely articulate, " You have seen it ? "

Mr. Mark gravely inclined his head.

" And is there any—" Clemence stopped short— she could not endure to put the question in such a form. " Is it not all cruel calumny ? " she faltered.

Mr. Mark hesitated. " The language is harsh and strong," was his guarded reply : it was too well comprehended by the miserable Clemence.

" When that—that money was settled," she stammered forth, without daring to look at her listener, " the house was safe, secure—there was no prospect of the ruin that followed ? "

" I believed so when I followed Mr. Effingham's directions. I, for one, had not the slightest doubt at that time of the solvency of the firm."

" And he—"

There was a long, painful silence ; Clemence heard nothing but the throbbing of her own heart. When the lady spoke again her tone was strangely altered ; there was in it no more of tremulous earnestness, but the calm resolution of despair.

" Mr. Mark, let me ask one more question. Is that money entirely at my own disposal ? "

" It is so by the terms of the settlement."

" Then I request you, acting in my name, to place the whole of it in the hands of the creditors."

"My dear madam—"

"My resolution is quite fixed," said Clemence, compressing her bloodless lips.

"But consider your position, that of the family—"

"I have resources of my own," replied Clemence firmly; "and my step-daughters are already provided for."

"You have resources?" repeated the lawyer doubtfully; "and the boy?"

"Shares whatever I have," answered Clemence.

"Perhaps a partial sacrifice," began Mr. Mark, but the lady interrupted him.

"All—all—I will give up all!"

"Not without reflection, dear madam, not on the impulse of the moment, not without consulting your friends."

"I consult you, the friend and adviser of my husband. Would not the act be a just one?"

"Just, perhaps, but—" and he paused.

"I have also consulted another friend, one who has been to me as a father—the Reverend Mr. Gray of Stoneby."

"And he advises this step?"

"I have not yet had time to receive his reply."

"Wait for it then," said the lawyer; "do nothing without beforehand weighing the consequences, or it is possible that you may regret even the noble and generous act, the thought of which does you honour."

After some further conversation, it was settled that Clemence should delay her decision until Mr. Gray's letter should be received, and then convey her final decision in writing to the man of business. Mr. Mark left her with a mingled sentiment of compassion and respect, which softened his usually abrupt manner to that of almost paternal tenderness.

"She has much to suffer, but she will suffer bravely," thought he, as he stepped into his brougham.

Clemence heaved a deep sigh when she found herself left alone. The spirit which had supported her through that painful interview now seemed to fail her. Very repugnant was it to her feelings to consult any one before her husband, on a point which concerned his honour so nearly. Could she not learn his will ere making so momentous a decision? To do so was the instinct of her heart, but not the judgment of her reason. No; even had she the means of communicating with Mr. Effingham, how could she seek guidance from him on the very path from which he had wandered? how ask him if it were her duty to counteract his own schemes, and clear, as far as possible, his character from a stain which he had deliberately contracted? It was, perhaps, better that a cloud of doubt should rest on what Mr. Effingham's ultimate wishes might be, and that Clemence should not behold in actual opposition her obedience to her husband and her duty to her God.

CHAPTER XX.

R. GRAY, as Clemence expected, viewed the subject of retaining or relinquishing the fortune in the same light that she did herself. He had, before answering her letter, seen the article in the *Times* which had so deeply wounded the young wife, and he had anticipated the resolution that she would form. The ideas of the simple-minded pastor were drawn, not from the maxims or example of the world, of which he indeed knew little, but from the pure, written Word of God. He read and believed that *the love of money* is *the root of all evil;* he read and believed that it is impossible *to serve God and Mammon;* and he had imbibed the spirit of that most solemn question, *What shall it profit a man if he gain the whole world and lose his own soul; or what shall a man give in exchange for his soul?*

The clergyman's letter was a very tender one.

full of pious consolation, and concluded by offering to the bankrupt's wife a home in the vicarage, where his dear partner, as well as himself, would ever regard her as a cherished daughter.

The good man's words were as balm to Clemence's wounded spirit, though she felt that her duty to her husband's family might render it impossible to accept an invitation which would otherwise have opened a harbour of refuge to her weary, storm-tossed soul. Clemence, without further delay, wrote her final decision to Mr. Mark. Never had she more impatiently despatched a letter than that which stripped her at once of the wealth which lay like a mountain's weight upon her conscience. Then, ringing the bell of the study—the room which she now almost exclusively occupied—Mrs. Effingham summoned, one after another, every member of her numerous household, and gave warning to all, without exception. It was a painful duty to the young mistress, but Clemence had nerved herself to its performance, and uttered a sigh of relief as the last of the servants quitted her presence. After all, it was easier to act than to think; the necessity for exertion was perhaps in itself a blessing.

Clemence, since reading the article in the *Times*, had secluded herself much from the family; she could not, in the first hours of her anguish, have endured the sight of familiar faces—the torture of being harassed with questions; she shrank even from the idea of sympathy, and could scarcely bear to look upon Vincent, the breathing image of one whom she thought of with grief, only exceeded by her love. Clemence felt it now, however, necessary to communicate with those whose interests were closely linked with her own, and to ascertain the views and feelings of her step-children before replying to the letter of Mr. Gray. With this view, mastering a strong sensation of repugnance, she ascended to the drawing-room, and found herself, on opening the door, in the presence of the assembled family.

Lady Selina was standing near the fire-place in earnest conference with Arabella; Vincent had stretched himself on the velvet rug, leaning upon his crossed arms in an attitude of thought, but he started up on his step-mother's entrance; Louisa lay on the sofa, her hand pressed over her eyes. There was a sudden break in the conversation when Clemence's form appeared, and Lady Selina, with a slow and stately air, advanced forward a few steps to meet her.

"Mrs. Effingham," she commenced, in tones even more cold and formal than usual, "I have been much surprised, greatly astonished to find that you have at once, without consulting any one, dismissed the whole of your husband's establishment! May I presume to ask your reason for so extraordinary a step ? "

" I cannot now afford to keep any such servants," replied Clemence, gently but firmly.

" Not afford!—really, Mrs. Effingham, your language is incomprehensible! Not afford, with sixty thousand pounds of your own in the funds!"

Clemence leaned on the table for support as she answered, " I will never touch a farthing of that money. I have given up all to the creditors, without reserve."

" That's right!" was the hearty exclamation of Vincent. Lady Selina stood for a moment actually speechless! Had she seen Clemence deliberately put an end to her own existence, the lady's amazement and horror could not have been greater.

" You have done such an insane thing !" she exclaimed at length.

" I have done it!" was the reply of Clemence.

" Then, madam, you have qualified yourself for Bedlam !" cried Lady Selina, condensed fury flashing from her eyes, all sense of what is due from one lady to another lost in the torrent of furious passion. " You have reduced your family to beggary ; you have subscribed to the condemnation of your own husband ; you have confirmed the opinion which I formed of you from the day when Mr. Effingham had the infatuation to throw himself away on a child —an idiot such as you ! "

"Aunt, you must not, you shall not—" cried Vincent ; but there was no staying the rushing flow of bitter words. Clemence endured them as the tree, whose leafy honours have been struck down by the woodman's axe, endures the pelting rain upon its prostrate form. It has felt the cold steel dividing its very core ; the sharp blow, the heavy fall, have been its fate ; the furious shower may now do its worst, it cannot lay it lower, any more than it has power to restore life to the withered foliage ! But when Lady Selina paused at length, mortified, perhaps, to find that her fiercest invectives could awake no answering flash of angry retort, Clemence quietly expressed her hope that she might be enabled so to economize as to live upon her limited resources without incurring debt.

"Resources !" exclaimed Lady Selina with ineffable contempt ; "the paltry interest of two or three thousand pounds, of which an hospital has the reversion ! If you can reduce yourself, madam, to such pauper allowance for the future, how extricate yourself from the meshes of present difficulties ? You speak of avoiding debt—you are in debt at the present moment to myself ! "

Clemence unclasped the massive bracelet on her

arm, and silently laid it on the table. It was her only reply. She then turned and quitted the apartment.

"I wish that she had flung it at aunt's head!" was Vincent's muttered comment on the scene.

A servant met Clemence as she was about to ascend the staircase. "Please, ma'am, Madame La Voye is at the door, and says that she must see you directly."

"Send her away," began Clemence, who felt as though her patience had already been tried to its utmost power of endurance; but as the man hesitated before again attempting a task in which he had already failed, she altered her resolution. "No; let her be shown into my room. Better meet this difficulty at once, and end it," murmured Clemence to herself, as the footman turned to obey.

Madame La Voye had, like all the rest of the world, heard of the bankruptcy of Mr. Effingham, and trembled for her unpaid bill. Her indignation had been inflamed to a high pitch by the article in the *Times*. Mr. Effingham she had denounced, and loudly, as a swindler, a cheat, and a felon; and she resolved, come what might, to have justice done to herself. She called at his house on Monday, and heard that Mrs. Effingham refused to see any one. Driven with difficulty from the door, the dressmaker repeated her call on the next day, with yet more fixed resolution to assert her claim. She would not be one of the miserable creditors who suffered themselves to be quietly robbed; she would not leave the house till she had received her money! Madame La Voye had worked herself up to an effervescence of indignation very unlike, indeed, to the smooth-tongued politeness with which she had received Mrs. Effingham into her show-apartments.

The Frenchwoman entered the house prepared to do battle for her rights, and the first words which she addressed to Clemence were abrupt almost to rudeness; but even she was in some degree awed by that pale, meek face, stamped with such deep impression of sorrow, and the first gentle tones of the silvery voice stilled her anger as if by a charm.

Clemence owned her debt and her inability to pay it ("Was all false, then, about the fortune?" thought La Voye); "But"—the lady hesitated and glanced at her wardrobe—"perhaps;" the Frenchwoman was not slow in comprehension—she spared the lady the humiliation of an explanation.

Pride was not Mrs. Effingham's besetting sin; but, in one form or other, perhaps no human heart is entirely free from it. It was painful to the lady to hear the value of her wardrobe estimated in her presence—repugnant to her feelings to hear this

mantle depreciated as no longer *à la mode*—that
dress, because the folds of the velvet had been slightly
ruffled in wearing.   Madame La Voye was not without a heart, and her anger had subsided into pity ;
but the coarseness of her nature appeared even in
what she intended for kindness, and in her compassion for the reduced lady she never for an instant
forgot self-interest.   Balancing, doubting, chaffering,
making a parade of "a wish to oblige," forming a
shrewd calculation that a beautiful Indian shawl,
"thrown into the lot, would make all even between
them," for almost an hour Madame La Voye made
her victim do bitter penance for a day's extravagance.
The mortifying interview, however, ended at last :
the Frenchwoman, well satisfied with her bargain,
quitted the house, and Clemence held in her hand,
receipted, that bill which had been the cause of so
much annoyance.

A sleepless night was passed in forming plans for
the future.   There had been only too much truth in
Lady Selina's words—how could the bankrupt's wife
find means to extricate herself from present difficulties?   Clemence's purse was empty.   The first instal-
ment of her income, miserable pittance as it appeared,
was not due to her for months; she had none to
whom to apply for assistance—none from whom she
could hope for relief.   Again and again Clemence

thought of her jewels, but they were all, with the exception of her watch, and a few trifles of little or no intrinsic worth, the gifts of her husband, and she regarded them almost as one in the Dark Ages might have regarded precious relics,—things far too valuable to be parted with, except with life. Yet there seemed to be no other resource, and Clemence now felt that in resigning all her fortune she had made a sacrifice indeed.

She rose sad and unrefreshed from her sleepless pillow, and yet a spirit of submission was shed into her heart. The iron had entered into her soul, but the wound was not poisoned by rebellious unbelief. Clemence was able to pray hopefully for her husband, and to trust that even the trials of his condition might be a means of drawing him nearer to his God. Surely the Almighty had judged his errors less severely than the harsh, unfeeling world? Had not those errors arisen from the very tenderness of his affection towards his wife? The temptations of prosperity had raised a mist around him ; the blast of misfortune had dispersed that mist, and the blue heaven would again smile above him ! Thus mused the young wife, her mind ever recurring to her absent lord as the centre of all its earthly thoughts. She could not see him, write to him, cheer him ; but she could still pour out her soul for him in prayer, and was there not sweet comfort in that ?

CHAPTER XXI

"THINK it right to lay before the children of my dear husband the course which I intend to pursue; their welfare is very near to my heart, and I cannot separate their interests from my own." Such were the words addressed by Clemence to Vincent and his sisters, while Lady Selina sat listening near, her face wearing a smile of cold scorn.

"I propose," continued Clemence, "to rent a cottage, a very small cottage in Cornwall, my native county, where necessary expenses can be reduced to a very narrow scale, unless I should receive directions from my husband which would induce me to alter my arrangements. If any of his family will share that humble abode, it will be my heart's desire to make them as—;" the word "happy" would not come, it died on the trembling lip, and a sigh concluded the broken sentence.

Arabella slightly elevated her brow and her shoulders; Louisa looked uneasily at her aunt.

"Such is your offer, madam; now listen to mine," said Lady Selina, folding her hands with the air of one about to give a proof of magnanimous self-denial. "I need not speak of the fervent affection which I have ever borne to my sister's children. My dear nieces have always looked to me as to the representative of a cherished mother, and in the hour of adversity I shall be the last to desert them. To my home, wherever that may be, most freely do I bid them welcome. With Vincent the case is different; though my love for him is the same, I cannot, as doubtless Mrs. Effingham will do, undertake the expenses of his education, or give to my dear nephew the advantages which are indispensable to a boy of his age."

Doubtless the affectionate aunt had not forgotten that whereas Vincent was absolutely penniless, the united incomes of her nieces, moderate as they were, would exactly double her own. Few of those who knew the lady intimately would have given her credit for disinterested kindness; but whatever might be her motive for the offer, Arabella was not slow to accept it.

"As, after what has occurred," said the proud girl, drawing herself up to her full height, "I should have

declined sharing a palace with Mrs. Effingham, her
society would scarcely allure me to the hovel which
she chooses as her place of abode.   I shall certainly
remain with my aunt."

But the choice of Louisa was not so readily made.
Her heart was drawn towards her step-mother, so
gentle and patient in her sorrow ; she felt for Clemence's loneliness and desolation.   Louisa could not
quite forget the tenderness with she had been tended
through her illness ; she could not quite forget how,
in the long dreary nights, a gentle watcher had
bathed her fevered brow, offered the cooling draught,
and spoken words of holy comfort and hope.   Her
step-mother was connected in her mind with all that
her conscience approved as right, her regret for past
errors, her resolutions of amendment, her thoughts
on religion and heaven.   Louisa had sufficient intelligence to see the difference of character between
Clemence and her aunt.   She could neither love nor
trust Lady Selina, as she could the pure-minded and
unselfish woman whom her father had chosen as his
wife.   But if Mrs. Effingham stood in the mind of
Louisa as the emblem and the representative of quiet
piety, her aunt, on the other hand, seemed that of the
world and all its tempting delights.   Lady Selina
would doubtless remain in London; to stay with her
was to partake of its pleasures, to enjoy its dazzling

scenes,—to dance, to shine, to see and to be seen. Oh! what magic images of glittering splendour were conjured up before the mind's eye of Louisa, by the name of a "London season!" And could she give up all this? could she endure to bury herself in dreary Cornwall, with no gaiety, no amusement, no admirers, like some flower doomed to—

> "Blush unseen,
> And waste its sweetness on the desert air?"

The idea was intolerable! Not gratitude, esteem, pity, conscience, were sufficient to fortify the poor girl against its terrors. She loved the world—she was of the world. Her idol had been shaken—but destroyed, never! It was resuming its old supremacy in a heart which, though apparently cleansed for a while, had been found empty of that divine faith which *overcometh the world!* Louisa hesitated, indeed, but not for long. Avoiding looking at her step-mother as she spoke, in a low, faltering voice, she said, "I think—I would rather—remain in London—like my sister."

Lady Selina cast a triumphant glance at Clemence, and going up to her nieces, embraced them both with many tender expressions, of which they, perhaps, guessed the real value. Mrs. Effingham quietly quitted the room, feeling very desolate and low, and thinking that for her the most welcome home would

be one much narrower and much quieter than any
cottage dwelling.   Just as she was entering her own
apartment, Vincent, who had been an excited though
silent listener to the preceding conversation, rushed
after and overtook her.   The boy flung his arms
tightly around her neck, exclaiming, "Mother! you
and I will stick together through thick and thin!"

Clemence returned the embrace with fervour; she
clasped the boy to her aching heart as if she would
have pressed him into it, and wept aloud in passionate grief, till almost choked by her convulsive sobs.
It was even as the accumulated masses of Alpine
snows, melting under the warm sunshine, burst
through the barriers which restrain them, and pour
their swelling floods into the valleys below.   Vincent was almost alarmed at the sudden violence of
emotion in one usually so quiet and gentle; but,
oh! what a weight of sorrow had been pent up in
that burdened heart!

Clemence was relieved by the burst of tears, and,
when again alone, seated herself before her desk,
and, resting her brow upon her hand, gave herself
up to thought.   Yes, she had something to live for!
That boy, that son of her heart, to him would she
devote her life, while the painful separation from his
father should last.   What Lady Selina had said on
the subject of Vincent's education, now pondered

over in solitude, wrought some change in the plans of Clemence. She must give up the idea of renting a cottage at Stoneby, where she could again enjoy the society of dear friends, and return to the occupations which she loved. Clemence could not, with justice to Vincent, undertake his tuition herself, and Mr. Gray was far too busily engaged in his extensive parish to do so. There was a market-town about ten miles from the village, where Clemence well knew that excellent daily tuition at an academy might be secured at a very trifling expense. This determined her course ; personal comfort and inclination should not for a moment be weighed against that which might be of such importance to the future prospects of her step-son. Clemence dipped her pen, and wrote an answer to the letter of Mr. Gray. She told him briefly of the part which she had taken in regard to the fortune ; declined with deep gratitude his offer of a home ; and entreated him, as soon as possible, to secure for her a cottage within walking distance of the academy of M———. Clemence limited the annual rent to a sum which would scarcely have paid for one of the dresses which she had worn in the days of her wealth, and requested that one of the girls from her Sunday school might be engaged as her solitary servant.

The descent into poverty is most painful when one

slow step after another is reluctantly taken down
the road of humiliation,—at each some cherished
comfort mournfully laid aside ! Better far to calculate at once the full amount of what must be resigned, put away every superfluity, and resolutely
make the plunge ! Clemence ended her letter by a
reiterated entreaty that her friend might engage
the cottage at his earliest convenience, as she yearned
to quit London, where every moment brought with
it some bitter pang of remembrance.

And now one other task remained to be performed
—a task intensely painful. Most thankfully would
Clemence have avoided it, or, if it must be fulfilled,
have deputed its execution to another. But to
whom could the young wife intrust the delicate office
of disposing of her jewels ? Was it absolutely
necessary to part with them at all ? Would none
of her friends, her numerous acquaintances, assist
her at least with a loan ? Clemence was sorely
tempted to try, and more than once commenced a
note to one whom she knew had the means to aid,
and whom she hoped might have also the heart ;
but she never got beyond the first line. Would it
be honest to borrow money, which she could hardly
hope ever to repay ? would it be right, while she
was in possession of valuables which might be con-
verted into gold ? After all, she could look on the

meditated sacrifice as made for her son, her Vincent, the child of her beloved husband, and that would give her courage to make it.

With a sickening heart Clemence removed from her jewel-box her husband's miniature, her mother's wedding-ring, and the little locket containing her parents' hair, which had been her bridal-gift from her uncle,—these, at least, she must ever retain ; and after a hasty preparation, as if fearful that her resolution might fail her if she should delay, even for an hour, the accomplishment of her design, Clemence glided out of her house with her jewel-case under her cloak.

Rapidly she walked through the streets, like one who dreads observation, drawing her thick black veil closely before her face. The shops in one of the principal throughfares of London, which it was her object to visit, were distant from Belgrave Square, and Mrs. Effingham had never before attempted to reach them on foot. She had repeatedly to inquire the road to them, and she did so with a shrinking timidity, which made more than one of her informants watch with an eye of instinctive pity her slight, fragile form, clad in its mourning garb, as it hurried on its onward way.

At length the gay, bright street was reached, noisy with carriages, thronged with pedestrians, offer-

ing in its thousand decorated windows temptations
for every eye.   Clemence had often driven down
that street in her own carriage, one of the fairest,
the most admired, the most envied of the throng.
Now, the bankrupt's wife dreaded the recognition of
any familiar face, as, weary and faint, she entered a
magnificent shop, which she had often noticed, in
passing, for the brilliant display of jewellery behind
its plate glass.

There were several customers in the shop, and Clemence, whose courage was failing her, was almost
upon the point of retreating, when the jeweller requested her to take a seat, she should be served in an
instant ; and Clemence sank wearily upon the proffered chair.   She had some time to wait.   A young
betrothed couple were choosing ornaments at the
counter.   At another time, the sight of their happiness would have only called forth emotions of pleasure ; but the painful contrast between their errand
and her own—they coming to purchase, she to part
with pledges of tender affection—was so overcoming
to Clemence, that when the jeweller at length, after
smilingly bowing out his customers, turned to inquire
her pleasure, she could scarcely command her voice
sufficiently to make her wishes intelligible.

The man's face at once lost its smiling expression.
" We sometimes exchange jewels," said he coldly

GOING TO SELL THE JEWELS. Page 203.

" but never make purchases in that way." Like a
fluttered bird, Clemence made her escape out of the
shop.

Must she try another ? Yes, that one on the
opposite side of the street. So engaged in her own
thoughts was Mrs. Effingham, so abstracted from all
that was passing around her, that as she crossed the
road she narrowly escaped being thrown down by a
passing vehicle. Once more summoning all her
resolution, she entered the shop. Here she was at
least attended to without delay. A tall, hard-visaged
man in spectacles, was ready to receive the lady's
commands. Clemence did not seat herself, but resting her trembling hand on the counter, told her
errand, and produced her jewels. The man opened
the case, and examined one article after the other,
as if mentally calculating its value. That precious
guard-ring, first gift of affection ; that chain which
loved hands had placed round her neck ; the diamond
brooch selected by her husband ; the watch, by
which she had counted so many blissful hours,—it
seemed to Clemence almost like desecration to see
them in the hand of a stranger ! It was really a
relief to her that a sum so much below their actual
value was offered by the jeweller, that she could,
without self-reproach, bear her treasures away from
the place.

And yet they must—they must be sold! She must not return to her home without success! A third time the drooping, heart-sick Clemence crossed the threshold of a shop, where everything spoke of luxury and wealth. This visit was the most trying of all! The dapper little tradesman behind the counter eyed with a quick and penetrating glance, not only the jewels, but their owner. Clemence read in his curious look, "How came you possessed of such things as these?" The bare idea of suspicion covered the pallid countenance of the youthful lady with a burning glow. It seemed to her as if the first words from the tradesman might be a question as to her own right to the property of which she wished to dispose. He spoke, but to Clemence's relief it was only to mention terms of purchase. Clemence, who had been tried almost beyond what she could bear, hastily closed with his offer, and again had to encounter that curious, scrutinizing look. Glad, most glad was she to leave the shop and the street, with their bustle and grandeur, far behind her, though the sum which she bore with her as the price of her jewels was less than one-third of what they had originally cost!

"But is the sacrifice sufficient?" Such was the question which Clemence asked herself as, almost sinking from fatigue, she at length regained the well-known precincts of Belgrave Square, and wearily remounted the steps of her magnificent mansion. "Is the sacrifice sufficient?" she repeated, as, hastily throwing off the cloak, whose weight even in that wintry day oppressed her, she sank on the sofa in her own apartment. Could she on so trifling a sum travel to Cornwall, and support Vincent and herself until she could draw her interest in June? It was barely possible that, by the severest economy, she might procure the necessaries of life, but Vincent's schooling, small as would be its expense—it would be idle to think of that! And was he, of whose talents and progress his father had been so proud, to lose by months of idleness all that he had gained during years of application? Clemence opened her desk, and drew from it her most precious possession—the miniature of her husband. Its diamond setting was even as the admiration and praise of the world which had once gathered around the original of that portrait, whom the same world now scorned and condemned. Would the picture be less precious without it, to her who valued every feature in the likeness beyond all the jewels in Peru? And yet fast fell the tears of the unhappy wife, as she removed from its sparkling encirclement the ivory from which her husband's eyes seemed to be looking upon her, calm and bright, as in the first happy days of their love! Could such a countenance deceive? Could dishonour ever sit on such a brow? Fervently Clemence pressed to her lips again and again the lifeless miniature, divested of outward adornment, but to its possessor even dearer than ever. Dearer, because there was nothing now but itself to give it value; dearer, because by man it would now be regarded as a worthless thing! —was it not an emblem of the beloved one whose image it bore?

CHAPTER XXII

COMING DOWN.

E will now change our scene, and pass over the events of more than a fortnight —a most weary fortnight to Clemence, who pined in vain for another letter from Mr. Effingham, and who dreaded that, by obeying what she considered to be the call of justice and conscience, she had drawn upon herself the displeasure of him whom she most desired to please.

The creditors, grateful for the noble disinterestedness which had preserved to them something from the wreck of their fortunes, were disposed to treat the bankrupt's wife with consideration and indulgence. She might remain in her present dwelling as long as it should suit her convenience to do so. But to Clemence, Belgrave Square was now a more intolerable abode than the wastes of Spitzbergen might have proved; to escape from it was to quit a prison, and she hastened her departure accordingly.

Lady Selina was also on the look-out for another abode, and spent the greater part of her time in house-hunting with Arabella ; Louisa was seldom of the party, as she shrank from exertion, and considered herself yet too delicate to be exposed to the wintry air.   During the fortnight before Clemence left London, Louisa was often her companion, and many a gentle word of counsel from the step-mother, whose misfortunes had rendered her dearer, sank into the poor girl's heart.   Lady Selina, whose pride was now undergoing perpetual mortifications—whose present occupation made her more bitterly feel the change in her fortunes, and more bitterly hate "the scrupulous idiot whose folly had plunged her whole family into distress," was so irritable and peevish, that Louisa sometimes asked herself whether, even in a worldly point of view, her choice had been a wise one.   She parted from Clemence with many tears, and with many promises of remembrance ;—like Orpah, she could weep for her Naomi,—but, like Orpah, she turned back to her idols.

It is a bright wintry evening.   The orb of the sun is just resting on a distant hill, and his reflected beams are lighting up the windows of a small cottage with a ruddy gleam ; the abode itself, however, has a lonely and rather desolate air.   It stands on an embankment which overlooks a railway whose straight dark lines form no picturesque object to the view, disappearing in the blackness of a tunnel which pierces a hill to the left. That hill, with its bare outline, entirely shuts out from sight the town of M——, distant about a mile from the spot. There is no appearance of any human habitation near, except this solitary little brick cottage, perched like a sentinel on the embankment, but turning its back to the railway, its front to the road, like one who prefers old friends to new, having probably been erected before the line was projected. The lone abode has a small, uncultivated garden in front, surrounded by a straggling fence, through whose sundry gaps an active child could easily force his way—from which a foot-path, seldom trodden, and green with moss, runs into the narrow road which leads to the town of M——.

There is, certainly, little to attract in the outward appearance of the dwelling, and within we shall find it furnished in the most plain and homely style. No carpet adorns the floor, no curtain breaks the straight line of the windows ; but the floor itself is spotlessly clean, the bright windows exclude none of the sun-beams, and a cheerful fire diffuses kindly warmth through the little white-washed parlour. The deal table is spread with a snowy cloth, and heaped with little dainties—nuts, oranges, and apples—brought by

Mr. Gray in a hamper carefully packed by his wife. A rosy-cheeked girl, about fifteen years old, is for the third time this day busily dusting the rush seats of the chairs, and altering their positions, so as to show them off to the best advantage. She stops in her employment every few minutes to run into the miniature kitchen and watch whether the chicken, likewise provided by Mrs. Gray, duly revolves before the fire. There are eggs, bacon, and cheese on the dresser, all produced from the Stoneby hamper, and the young servant looks with admiration on her own preparations for the feast.

A proud, rich, and happy girl Martha Jones feels herself this day to be ! Is it not wondrous promotion to be sole servant to such a lady as Mrs. Effingham, —to take the place of so many footmen dressed more dashingly than militia officers,—a housekeeper who, as she has heard, looks much grander than Mrs. Gray —and a bevy of fine London maids ! And a whole sovereign every quarter ! is not that wealth to one who has never touched a gold piece in her life ? Can any service be more delightful than that of sweet, gentle " Miss Clemence," who has always a kind word for every one, and never willingly gives trouble or pain ! Martha envies the lot of no queen as she cheerfully goes about her work, the joyousness of ner blithe young heart often breaking forth into song.

R-r-r-r-r! with a roar a train rushes past, and vanishes into the dark chasm of the tunnel, before the cottage has ceased to tremble or the windows to rattle with the vibration! Martha, unaccustomed to the sound, starts as if she were shot, then bursts into a merry laugh.

"How it makes one jump! I thought as how the house would come down! I'd as lief not live quite so near a railway! But I'll get used to it, no doubt; and they say, as the trains come in so reg'lar, they'll serve instead of a clock. Missus must be a-travelling by that train; she'll get to the town in no time. She'll be gladsome to find Mr. Gray at the station, all ready to welcome her back. They say, poor dear lady, she's had a deal of trouble since that merry day of the wedding, when we had such a feast on the green. First there was the good old captain drowned, and she was the light of his eyes—I guess there was no love lost atween them; then her money ran away. How it went at once I can't make out. Mr. Effingham seemed to have no end of it when he married! Had we not each of us a warm winter's cloak, and Mr. Gray a silver inkstand! and did not Mr. Effingham's gentleman tell the clerk as how his master was wondrous rich, and lived in a palace in Lunnon, whose very stables were bigger than the parsonage, and that he would spend as much at one

dinner as would build us a new church-tower! It'll
be a mighty change to Miss Clemence," soliloquized
the girl, her merry, good-humoured face assuming a
graver expression as she looked around her; "certain,
things are very different here from what they was
even in the captain's cottage. She made everything
so pretty around her! But so she will here; we
shan't know the place when she's been here a month!"
quoth the light-hearted Martha, as she arranged
for the last time in a saucer of white crockery some
six or seven early violets discovered after much
search by the school-children at Stoneby, and sent as
tokens of affection to their former dear young teacher.
Surely the perfume of those wild-flowers would not
have been sweeter had they been placed in a vase of
Sévres china!

The sun had now entirely disappeared, though a red
glow remained on the horizon. Martha became more
and more impatient. Even at the hazard of spoiling
the dinner, she could not help running to the little
broken gate at the end of the garden, to see if any
one were coming up the road.

"Surely they'll take the evening coach; Mr. Gray
must return in it to Stoneby, or he'll not get back
to-night. 'Twill drop 'em just at the gate. Was
not that the sound of wheels? Yes! surely! and
there's the coach turning the corner!—and—I've

never cut the bacon ready for frying, and the chicken will be burned to a coal!"

Back flew the little maid to her post of duty, busy, bustling and happy as a bee in a clump of heather; and she returned to the gate just in time to see Mr. Gray bending from the top of the coach to give a last word and blessing to Clemence, while Vincent assisted, with more good-will than strength, to haul down a corded box and portmanteau.

Clemence stood for some moments with clasped hands and swimming eyes, watching the coach as in the darkening twilight it rattled away, bearing from her the only friend upon earth who had given her ready assistance and counsel in this her time of adversity and trial. How gladly would she have accompanied the pastor to the dear village where her happy childhood had been spent! Vincent was too busy to watch his step-mother. He felt as self-important in charge of the luggage as if all the wealth that his father had ever possessed had been intrusted to his sole care.

"Here, you—what's your name, little girl!" he cried to Martha, "just help me in with this box. Is not the servant there to uncord it?" Clemence turned at the sound of his voice, and her kindly greeting to the smiling, courtesying Martha, first announced to Vincent that the "little girl" was actually the servant who was to comprise in herself all the establishment of Willow Cottage.

Vincent was young and merry-hearted, and as he helped to drag the portmanteau into the cottage, and looked at its white-washed walls and bare floor, so unlike everything to which he had been accustomed, the idea of actually dwelling in such a place struck him as irresistibly comic.

"I say, mamma!" he exclaimed with a laugh, "are we really to live in this nut-shell? How amazed Aunt Selina would be could she see it! It's just like a gardener's cottage!"

"As we can't turn the cottage into a palace to suit Master Vincent," said Clemence, with a desperate attempt at cheerfulness, "suppose that Master Vincent turn into a gardener to suit the cottage?"

"I think that I must turn into a great many other things besides—cook, for instance," he added, as Martha placed the roasted chicken upon the table; "I think that we must call that a *black cock!*"

Clemence silenced the boy by a glance till the poor girl had quitted the room, and then Vincent laughingly exclaimed, "Why, I was making game of the chicken, and not of the cook! but could we not give her a hint not to roast a poor fowl to a cinder next time?"

Clemence thought, "It will be long enough before we have another fowl to roast!"

Notwithstanding the inexperience of the cook, Vincent, whose appetite was sharpened by fatigue and cold, did ample justice to the feast which Mrs. Gray had provided, and ate half of the chicken himself, to say nothing of bacon and eggs. He vainly endeavoured to induce his step-mother to follow his example.

"I say," observed Vincent, busy with a wing, "that girl is a capital servant, I dare say, and Mrs. Ventner is not fit to hold a candle to her; but I wish that she knew how to hold a candle to us! Just see!—she has forgotten to bring us any, and has left her own tallow dip, to 'make darkness visible,' as papa would say."

"My dear boy," replied Clemence quietly, "we must not look for better light here, till we have the sun himself as our candle."

"A *dip* into poverty; but we'll *make light of it!*" cried Vincent, the pun reconciling him to the privation. Whether exhilarated by change of air, or desirous to cheer his companion, the boy seemed disposed to make a jest of every discomfort. There was in him a buoyancy of spirit, an energy of will, which had never appeared to such advantage in the pampered child of the wealthy banker.

"But, I say, we must make ourselves a little more comfortable!" cried Vincent; "the wind blows through that window like a gale, and Martha has forgotten to close the shutters!" Up he sprang to remedy her negligence. "Why, there's not a bit of a shutter!" he exclaimed in surprise; "nothing at all to keep the wind out!"

"I think that you will have to make some," said Clemence.

"Make shutters!" exclaimed Vincent, look doubtful at first whether to be pleased or disgusted, but deciding at last on the former. "Well, it's lucky I brought my tool-box. I never did anything but spoil wood as yet, but maybe I'll turn out a capital carpenter, if I mayn't be a cook. I'll saw away at my shutters in the evening when I come back from my studies." Then in a softer tone Vincent went on: "Won't you be very dull here all alone during the day? what will you do to amuse yourself here?"

"I have provided myself, dear boy, with plenty of occupation. I found, before we left London, that you required new shirts, so I have brought a supply of the material with me that I may make them myself."

"You make my shirts!" exclaimed Vincent with feeling; "well, I shall like them better than any that ever I wore. I'm growing quite proud, you see, now that I've such a lady for my needle-woman!"

"And I quite grand," replied Clemence, with a smile, "when I've such a gentleman for my carpenter!"

With such light conversation the weary, heart-stricken wife strove to beguile the first evening in Willow Cottage. Whatever her own secret sorrows might be, she was resolved that they should not sadden her intercourse with Vincent. It was a pleasure to her to see the brave cheerfulness with which he was preparing to do battle with difficulties. With his bright eyes and ringing laugh, Vincent was to his step-mother the impersonification of Hope. And never had Clemence with more fervent thankfulness pronounced the grace after meals, than in that small, cold, and comfortless cottage, for which she had exchanged all the luxuries of her splendid mansion. She had resigned those luxuries for the dearer one of eating her bread in peace, and with a quiet mind, conscious of wronging none; and sweeter, oh! how much sweeter, would be the poorest crust partaken of thus, than all the dainties of a board at which it were mockery to ask a blessing!

CHAPTER XXIII

INCENT was much too weary that night to notice whether his bed were soft, and slept in luxurious repose till the morning light awoke him. Dressing quickly, he entered the little parlour where Clemence was preparing the breakfast. She greeted him with a cheerful smile. "We have not the fatigue of stairs here," she observed.

"And we've the advantage of hearing at one end of the house everything that passes at the other," said Vincent;—"while I was dressing I did not lose a note of the song that Martha was singing in the kitchen. I think that there was an earthquake last night, or else I dreamed that I felt one."

"It was a train passing," said Clemence; "it was too dark yesterday when we arrived for us to notice how close to our house the line runs."

"So half-a-dozen times a day we'll have the

earthquake of Lisbon, without paying our shilling—
so much to treat the ear; and as for the eye—is
there anything in the Royal Academy brighter than
that famous patch-work table-cover, which I see
displayed in all its glory? I'm sure that you are
determined to make our cottage gay with every
colour of the rainbow!"

The mind of Clemence was wandering to graver
subjects. How the anxious wife pined for a letter
with the foreign post-mark! It came not, and her
heart was full of uneasy forebodings, which she
struggled, however, to hide from her young companion. Clemence even chatted merrily with the
boy, as, after herself putting up the dinner which
he was to carry with him to M——, she accompanied him to the town, to introduce him to his
new master. Clemence was not aware that an
entrance fee had been required, still less that it had
been already paid from the slender purse of her
friend, Mr. Gray.

In quiet routine sped the lives of Clemence and
Vincent; the simple meal, the social prayer, the
reading the Word of consolation, ever preceding
hours of busy study to the one—to the other a long
day of quiet occupation and anxious thought. The
evening was always cheerful; Vincent returned
home full of all that had happened either to himself

or his companions, and made his step-mother laugh
at his tales out of school. She knew all the fun
that the boys had had at football, and the hopes of
a famous cricket-match to come off between M——
and B——. With pleasant converse and plenty of
occupation, no wonder that Vincent cared not that
the evening meal was but a basin of porridge. The
pressure of poverty, indeed, fell far more heavily on
the lady, whose health had been much shaken by
sorrows, and who required the comforts which a
rigid sense of duty induced her to deny herself.
All her ingenuity was taxed to prevent Vincent
from feeling its weight. Little did he dream that
the fire which blazed so merrily in the evening was
never kept in during the day, that the small stock
of fuel might be husbanded; and that when the
chill of the parlour was no more to be endured,
Mrs. Effingham carried her work to the kitchen for
the sake of its kindly warmth. Little did he dream
how different the meal which was packed up so
neatly for him every morning, was from that which
his kind provider reserved for herself in the cottage,
till one day Vincent unexpectedly made his appearance in the parlour two or three hours earlier than
usual.

"The academy's broken up!" he cried, as he
entered, "and when we shall meet again no one can

say. There are three cases of scarlet fever amongst the boys!"

"Not alarming ones, I trust?" said Clemence.

Vincent went on without appearing to notice the question. "So I'd better begin the profession of gardener at once, and learn about English roots instead of Greek ones. As I knew I'd be back in time for dinner, I gave my sandwiches away to a beggar—I prefer something hot in such weather as this! But how's this?" he continued, seating himself at the table: "you've come to your cheese-course already!"

"Did you consider meat as a matter of course?" said Mrs. Effingham playfully, as she cut a slice of bread for her unexpected guest.

"You don't mean to say that you are going to dine upon nothing but bread and cheese?"

Clemence only smiled in reply.

"And what was your dinner yesterday?"

"Nay, I am not going to let you into the secrets of my establishment," Mrs. Effingham gaily answered.

"And the fire's out!"

"We shall try your skill in re-lighting it, dear Vincent," said his mother.

The boy gazed thoughtfully into her pale thin face, and for the first time since he had come to Willow Cottage, Vincent heaved a sigh. "Poverty is a trial—a great trial," was his silent reflection; " but when I am old enough to earn my own living and hers, she shall never know its bitterness more."

Clemence regretted less the pause in her step-son's attendance at school, as the weather had become unusually severe. Winter, who for a few days had seemed on the point of yielding up his empire to his smiling successor, now with fiercer fury than ever resumed his iron sway. Standing-water froze even within the cottage, the windows were dim with frost, the little garden was one sheet of snow, and even the postman made his way with difficulty along the road. It was seldom that he stopped at the gate of Willow Cottage, and he never did so without sending a thrill of hope, not un-mingled with fear, through the bosom of Clemence Effingham. The morning after the breaking up of the academy he brought a letter for Vincent.

"It is Louisa's hand," called out the boy, as he tramped back through the snow to the cottage door, at which Clemence was impatiently waiting; "I'm glad that she has answered my note at last. She is such a lazy girl with her pen!"

"Come and read it comfortably by the fire," said his step-mother, concealing her own disappointment.

"*Pro bono publico*, I suppose, you and I being all the public at hand." Vincent threw himself down in front of the cheerful blaze. "Now for a young lady's epistle—written on dainty pink paper and perfumed—to be given with sundry notes and annotations by the learned Vincent Effingham :—

"My dear Vincent,

"You ask me how I like our new house. What a question! Beaumont Street after Belgrave Square! I feel as if I were imprisoned in a band-box! [I wish she could see our cottage!] Our grand piano blocks up half our sitting-room—a miserable relic of grandeur, which only serves to incommode us, since none of us have the heart to touch it. The furniture of the house is wretched —fancy chintz-covered chairs and a horse-hair sofa! [Fancy rush-bottomed chairs, and no sofa at all!] Aunt Selina is in shocking spirits [alias temper], has not appetite for food [while we have not food for our appetite], and is always painfully recurring to the past. Our horse—you know we have now only one—has fallen lame [a misfortune which can't happen to us]; and, as Arabella says that she detests walking, I am quite shut up in the house. It is dull work looking out of the window, with nothing for view but the brick houses on the opposite side of the street, scarce anything passing but those wretched grinding organs which murder my favourite opera airs! It is strange how our friends seem to have forgotten us : we have hardly a visitor here. I suppose that this is caused by the change in our position—which gives one a very bad opinion of the world. But I hope that things may look brighter when this long, miserable winter is past, and the London season commences.

"Pray give my love to dear Mrs. Effingham. I miss both her and you very much. I am sure that she will let me know if she receive any tidings of papa."

*　　*　　*　　*　　*

"Well!" exclaimed Vincent, as he folded up the note, and replaced it in its rose-tinted envelope, "I would rather leave the world as we have done, than find out that the world was leaving me!"

CHAPTER XXIV.

DARKNESS AND DANGER.

S Martha on the next morning took in the breakfast, she told her mistress with a look of alarm that she had just heard from the baker that the scarlet fever was making rapid progress in M——. Many had died from its effects; amongst them two of the boys who had been attending classes in the academy.

As Martha retailed her tidings, Clemence noticed that Vincent turned pale.

" Did you hear the boys' names ? " he asked hastily.

" I think, sir, as one was the curate's eldest son."

" Ah, poor Wilson ! " exclaimed Vincent with feeling; " and to think that but three days ago he was sitting at my side, laughing and joking, as strong and as merry as any boy in the school ! "

" They says," observed Martha, always glad of an

opportunity to gossip,—"they says that the fever be raging in a terrible way. There's been three children carried off in one house, and now the mother's a-sickening. The baker says 'tis just like the plague; people die a'most before they've time to know they be ill!"

"I wonder if my turn will come next," said Vincent, as Martha quitted the little parlour. "I had the place next to Wilson in the class, and we were wrestling together on the green. Oh, don't look so frightened," he added more cheerfully, "there's nothing the matter with me now."

He walked to the window and looked out, having scarcely tasted his breakfast. "Did you ever see such a day!" he exclaimed; "the snow falls, not in flakes, but in masses! I don't believe that the coach will be able to run. There were three horses to it yesterday; they could scarcely drag it along, and snow has been falling ever since. One would be glad of a little sunshine. I think that this winter never will end!"

Vincent remained so long listlessly watching the snow, that Clemence at last suggested that he should read to her a little, while she would go on with her work. Vincent, with a yawn, consented; but though the book had been selected for its power of entertaining, this day it did not seem to amuse.

Vincent did not read with his wonted spirit, and soon handed over the volume to Clemence.

Mrs. Effingham read a few pages, and then suddenly stopping, looked uneasily at her boy. He was leaning his brow on his hand, and closing his eyes as if in thought or in pain.

"You are unwell, my Vincent!" she exclaimed.

"Oh, I'm all right," was the nonchalant reply.

"The death of his young companion has naturally saddened his spirits. God grant that this depression have no other cause!" was the silent thought of the step-mother.

She read a little longer, and stopped again. "Indeed, my son, you do not look well!" Clemence rose and laid her hand upon his forehead—it was feverish and hot to the touch.

"Well, I do not feel quite as usual," owned Vincent, scarcely raising his heavy eyelids. "I've such a burning feeling in my throat."

Clemence's heart sank within her; she knew the symptom too well. Trembling with an agonizing dread lest another fearful trial of submissive faith might be before her, she yet commanded herself sufficiently to say, in a tone that was almost cheerful, "I see that I must exert my authority, and order you off to bed."

"Do you think that I have taken the fever?" said Vincent, rising as if with effort.

"Whether you have taken it or not, you can be none the worse for a little precaution, and a little motherly nursing," she added, putting her arm fondly around the boy.

As soon as Clemence had seen Vincent in his room, she flew with anxious haste to the kitchen. "Martha!" she cried, but in a voice too low to reach the ear of her step-son, "you must go directly to M—— for Dr. Baird. He lives in the white house on the right, next the church. Beg him to come without a minute's delay; I fear that Master Vincent has caught the fever! Go—no time must be lost!"

The kind-hearted girl appeared almost as anxious, and looked more alarmed than her mistress. Having repeated her directions, Clemence returned to the small apartment of Vincent. He was sitting on the side of his little bed, one arm freed from his jacket, but apparently with too little energy to draw the other out of its sleeve. His head was heavy and drooping, and an unnatural flush burned on his cheek. He passively yielded himself up to his step-mother's care, and soon was laid in his bed. Before an hour had elapsed Vincent was in the delirium of fever, the scarlet sign of his terrible malady overspreading every feature!

How helpless Clemence felt in her loneliness then!
Not a human being near to suggest a remedy or
whisper a hope! She waited and watched for the
doctor, till impatience worked itself up to torture.
Why did he delay, oh, why did he delay, when life
and death might hang on his coming! A train
passed, and Clemence started, though by this time
well accustomed to the sound. Amongst all the
human beings—living, loving human beings—who
passed in it so close to her cottage, there was not
one to pity or to help—not one who could even
guess the anguish and danger overshadowing the
lone little dwelling!

Clemence's only comfort was to weep and to pray
by the bed-side of her suffering boy. He could
neither mark her tears nor hear her prayers; he lay
all unconscious of the love of her who would so
gladly have purchased his life with her own.

At last hope came; there was a sound at the
door! With rapid but noiseless step Clemence
glided from Vincent's room to meet the doctor so
anxiously expected. Martha stood at the threshold,
stamping off the snow which hung in masses to her
shoes. Bonnet, cloak, and dress were all whitened
with the storm; but notwithstanding the bitter
cold, heat-drops stood on the brow of the girl.

"Is he coming?" gasped Clemence.

Martha burst into tears. "O ma'am, I've done all that I could. I've been battling against it this hour! I'm sure I thought I'd be buried in the snow!"

"The doctor!—the doctor!" cried Clemence, impatiently.

"I could not get as far as M——. The way's blocked up with the snow. Sure, ma'am, I did my best."

Clemence clasped her hands almost in despair. Then her resolution was taken. "Watch by my son; do not quit him for an instant. I will go for the doctor myself."

"It's impossible! quite impossible!" cried the girl. "I sank up to the knee every step. You'll be lost, oh, you'll be lost in the snow!" Her last words were unheard by Clemence, who had already commenced her brief preparations for encountering the storm.

Can love, strong as death, enable that slight, fragile form to force its way through the piled heaps of snow which block up and almost obliterate the path? Can it give power to the young, delicate woman to face such a blast as strips the forest trees of their branches, and levels the young pines with the sod? For a short space Clemence struggles on, the fervour of her spirit supplying the deficiency

in physical strength ; but every yard is gained by
such an effort, that she feels that her powers must
soon give way.   She could as well try to reach
London as M.——   In her agony she cries aloud—
"O my God! my God! have pity upon me!" and
when was such a cry, wrung from an almost breaking and yet trusting heart uttered to the Father of
mercies in vain ?

Clemence cast a wild gaze around her.   Almost
parallel with the road, and at no great distance from
it, a long break in the wide dreary waste of snow
marked the course of the railway.   Clemence turned
to the right, by instinct rather than reflection, made
her difficult way to the top of the bank, and gazed
down on the cutting below.   Snow there was on it,
indeed, but the line of communication was too important for it to be suffered to accumulate there in
such heaps as on the comparatively unfrequented
road.   Within the tunnel itself all would, of course,
be clear.   A desperate thought flashed on the soul
of Clemence.   One way was open to her still,—a
way dark and full of terrors, but one by which
M—— might yet be gained, and assistance brought
to her suffering boy !   She gave herself no time for
reflection, but scrambling, stumbling, slipping down
the bank, soon found herself on the side of the line, half
buried by the snow carried with her in her descent.

ENTERING THE TUNNEL.

Page 217.

Clemence made a few steps, and then paused and shuddered. Before her was the opening of the tunnel—dark, dreadful as a yawning grave. Could she venture to enter its depths—perhaps to be there crushed beneath the next passing train? Were any trains expected at this time? Clemence pressed her forehead, and tried to remember. One she had heard within the hour—of that at least she was certain—the up-train to London, she believed. But the state of the railway had delayed all traffic; and it was impossible for Clemence to calculate exactly the chances of a coming train. The idea of being met or overtaken by one was too terrible for the mind to dwell on. The risk was too great to be run. Clemence, marvelling at her own temerity in having entertained the thought for a moment, turned round to go back to her home. But the sight of her own lone cottage on the summit of the bank made her hesitate once more. Before her mind floated the image of her beloved boy dying for want of that assistance which it might be in her power to bring; then that of her husband in the anguish of his grief for his own—his only son! Again Clemence turned, her face almost as white as the snow falling fast around her. Clasping her hands in prayer, with her eyes raised for a moment to the lowering sky above, she faintly murmured the words,

"*Though I walk through the valley of the shadow of death I will fear no evil, for Thou art with me;*" then rousing all her courage for the desperate attempt, she entered the gloomy tunnel.

No lingering step there—no doubting, hesitating heart! as with the painful duties which conscience had before imposed upon her shrinking nature, Clemence felt a necessity to *go through*, and through as quickly as possible. She hastened on as rapidly as the darkness would permit, guiding herself by the wall, and the daylight at the end, which gleamed before her like a large, pale star. The timid woman wished to place, as soon as might be, such a distance between herself and the spot where she had entered, that she might feel it as dangerous to return as to proceed. She sped on her way, scarcely daring to think, keeping her eye on that increasing star, till it was needful to pause to take breath. The air was thick, clammy, and unwholesome—Clemence felt it like a shroud around her, as she stood in that living grave. "Oh, shall I ever be in daylight again?" she exclaimed, with the horror of darkness upon her. Her foot was on one of the iron lines; she thought that she felt a vibration—was it not the wild fancy of her excited brain? It was sufficient to make the very blood seem to curdle in her veins, and to absorb all her senses in the one act of listening.

Yes!—yes!—yes!—the low, distant rumble that she knows too well,—it comes from behind, from the London down-train; the horror of death is to Clemence concentrated in each terrible moment, as, almost petrified with fear, she turns round to gaze! A fiery red eye gleams through the darkness; the light from the entrance is almost blocked out; the rumble becomes a hollow roar, ever growing louder and louder; and, with a wild shriek of terror, Clemence falls senseless to the earth!

CHAPTER XXV.

THE SEARCH.

THREE gentlemen are travelling from London on that dreary wintry day. They occupy the same carriage in the train, but are personally unknown to each other. Two of them, a lawyer and a railway director, soon break through the cold reserve which marks an English traveller. A proffered newspaper, a remark on the weather, and they have launched into the full tide of conversation on railway speculations, foreign politics, and the future prospects of the nation.

The third passenger, a grave and silent man, sits in a corner of the carriage with his hat drawn low over his brow, keeping company only with his own thoughts, which seem to be of no agreeable nature. The mind of Effingham—for it is he—is in harmony with the gloomy, wintry scenes through which he is passing. He has but yesterday arrived from France, his case having been carried through the bankruptcy court during his absence. He has this morning had an interview in London with his daughters and Lady Selina.

Clemence's decision in regard to the fortune so carefully secured to her by her husband at the expense of honour and conscience, had wakened a wild tumult of feeling in the breast of the unhappy bankrupt. Anger, shame, surprise, not unmingled with secret approbation, had struggled together in Effingham's soul. Early impressions had been revived there —impressions made when his young heart had been guileless as his son's was now, when he would have shrunk from dishonour as from a viper, and have as lief touched glowing metal as a coin not lawfully his own! It had needed a long apprenticeship to the world to efface these early impressions, or rather, to render them illegible, by writing above them the maxims of that wisdom which is foolishness with God. Effingham was perhaps the more irritated against his wife, because he had sufficient conscience left to have a secret persuasion that she had only done what was right—returned that to its lawful possessors which never ought to have been hers. The difficulty, rather the shame, which he felt in expressing his feelings on the subject, had prevented him from writing at all.

It was while still enduring this mental conflict—
now accusing Clemence of romantic folly, now con-
demning himself on more serious grounds—that
Effingham, on his return from France, had a meeting with Lady Selina. A visit to Beaumont Street,
under existing circumstances, was little likely to
soothe the proud man's irritated feelings. Lady
Selina neglected nothing that could make him more
painfully aware of the change in the circumstances
of his family. She artfully sought to revenge herself upon Clemence, by bringing that change before
the eyes of her husband, not as the result of his
own wild speculations, but as caused by the obsti-
nate folly of one who presumed to be more scrupulous than her lord, and who followed her own
romantic fancies rather than the advice of experienced friends. Arabella followed in the track of
her aunt ; while Louisa's drooping looks and tearful
eyes did more, perhaps, than the words of either, to
increase Effingham's displeasure towards his wife.
He set out on his long journey to Cornwall full of
bitterness of spirit, attempting to turn the turbid
tide of emotion into any channel rather than that
of self-condemnation.

Effingham remained, therefore, moody and abstracted, while his companions chatted freely together
on subjects of common interest, till the entrance of

the train into a tunnel caused that pause in conversation which a change from light to sudden darkness usually produces.

"What was that sound!" exclaimed Effingham.

"The whistle," shortly replied his next neighbour, immediately resuming his discourse with the gentleman opposite, while Effingham relapsed into silence.

"We must be nearly an hour behind time!" observed the lawyer, looking at his watch by the light of the lamp.

"Impossible to keep to it—state of the roads—never knew such a season!" was the director's reply. "You saw the signal as we passed; the rest of the trains will be stopped; no more travelling till the lines are cleared."

"I hear that a stage-coach in the north had actually to be dug out of the snow," said the other.

As the observation was uttered, the train burst again into the open daylight, and in a few minutes more the black, hissing engine was letting out its steam at the station of M——.

Effingham sprang out of the carriage, and proceeded immediately to make inquiries as to the direction of Willow Cottage. Hearing that the distance was not great, and judging that it would be less difficult to make his way over the snow on

foot than in any conveyance, he left his portmanteau, with directions that it should be forwarded
after him, and set out at once for the cottage.

The snow-shower had ceased, and the wind was
on his back, therefore, though sinking deep at every
step, the strong man made his way through the
obstacles which had proved insurmountable to Clemence. His thoughts were so painfully engaged,
that those obstacles were scarcely heeded. On he
pressed with gloomy resolution, making, however,
extremely slow progress, till, on passing a bend of
the road, he came in sight of the little lone cottage.

"It is impossible that Clemence can be living in
that miserable hovel; and yet, by the description,
the cottage can be none other than this!" exclaimed
Effingham, surveying the tenement with mingled
surprise and displeasure.

At this point the snow lay so thick on the path,
that Effingham found it very difficult to proceed;
but the goal was near, and by main strength he
forced his way over and through the drifted heaps.
Suddenly an object on the road before him arrested
his attention. Almost close to Clemence's little
gate, a horse, which had fallen floundering amongst
the heavy masses, was struggling to his feet; and
his rider, whose shaggy great-coat, almost covered
with snow gave him the appearance of a Siberian

bear, was encouraging the efforts of the animal both by voice and rein. Effingham redoubled his exertions, in order to give aid to the stranger; but before he could reach the spot, horse and horseman had risen from the snow.

"Thank you, sir; no harm done!" said the rider to Effingham, patting the neck of his panting steed. "No danger of broken bones with such a soft bed to receive us. But I don't see how I'm ever to get back to M———. It's unlucky, for I've plenty of patients there anxious enough to see me. I was sent for in great haste this morning by an old gentleman who lives some way off. I expected to find him in extremity, and it turned out to be nothing worse than a fit of the gout! I wish that I'd prescribed him a three miles' ride through the snow!" The doctor shook his broad shoulders and laughed.

"What will you do now?" said Effingham.

"Do! I can neither get backward nor forward, so I suppose I must stay where I am. Lucky there's that cottage so near; for though there's no sign up that I can see, doubtless I shall find in my extremity 'good entertainment for man and beast.'"

"The cottage, sir, is mine," said Effingham stiffly; then added, with his natural graceful politeness, "I am sure that whatever accommodation it may afford will be very much at your service."

Before the doctor had time to reply to one whose appearance and demeanour so little corresponded with that of his dwelling, Martha came running breathlessly to the gate. "O sir, I'm so thankful to see you!" she exclaimed; "but haven't you brought back my mistress with you?"

"Here's a riddle to read!" cried the doctor gaily, turning with a smile to Effingham; but the husband had caught alarm from the anxious, excited face of the servant.

"What's the matter?" he sternly exclaimed.

"Master Vincent is bad with the fever, and mistress—surely, sir, she sent you here?" added Martha, turning anxiously towards the doctor.

"No, my good girl, I've seen no lady."

"Oh! mercy! mercy!" cried Martha, wringing her hands; "then maybe she never got through the tunnel!"

"The tunnel!" exclaimed Effingham, with a start of horror; "for mercy's sake, girl, explain yourself!'"

"Master Vincent is ill, and mistress went herself for the doctor," replied the trembling Martha, terrified both by his tone and his eye. "She could not get on through the snow; I saw her slide down the bank there; I saw her go into the tunnel."

The words seemed to scar Effingham's brain.

Without waiting to hear more, with the gesture of a madman he rushed forward, as if impelled by irresistible impulse, to fly to the succour of his wife. Then he suddenly stopped, and called loudly for a torch.

"There's no torch, but,—but a lantern."

"Bring it, for the love of Heaven!" cried the miserable husband. The girl flew to obey, while he stood almost stamping with fierce impatience, as if every moment of delay were spent on the rack.

"My dear sir," began the compassionate doctor,—

He was interrupted by Effingham, who said, in a hoarse, excited tone, "My boy, she says, is ill. Providence has brought you here; see to him— save him! I—I have a more terrible mission to perform! O God! preserve my brain from distraction!"

Martha brought the lantern after a brief absence, which seemed to the husband interminable. He snatched it from her hand, with the question, which his bloodless lips had hardly the power to articulate, "Did any train pass after she left this place?"

"Yes; *one!*"

Without uttering another word Effingham sprang forward on his fearful quest.

The snow displaced on the top of the bank and

down its side, and the scattered flakes on the cutting below, served but as too sure guides. To plunge down the steep descent was the work of a moment. Effingham was now upon the line where not two hours previously Clemence had stood and trembled. The blackness of the opening before him recalled to him, with a sense of unutterable horror, the cry which had pierced his ear in the tunnel. Effingham loved his young wife—fondly, passionately loved. If any emotion of displeasure towards her were remembered in that awful hour, it was but to intensify the anguish of remorse. He felt himself to be a wretch marked by the justice of Heaven for the keenest torment that mortal can bear and live. Loss of fortune, friends, fame —what was all that to the misery which he might now be doomed to endure! He might find her —his loved, his beautiful Clemence, the pride of his life, the treasure of his heart—oh, how he might find her he dared not think. On he pressed, the dim light from his lantern gleaming on the cold iron below, the stony walls, the damp, dripping roof; but there was yet no sign of a human form.

Effingham called aloud. The dreary arches resounded with the much-loved name; their hollow echoes were the only reply. There! surely there is some object dimly seen through the gloom,—a dark mass lying straight before him! With one bound Effingham is beside it, on his knees, trembling like an aspen, then sobbing like a child! That is no crushed and mangled form that he clasps; cold, indeed, and still, it lies in his arms, but there is breath on the lip and pulsation in the heart. "She lives! God be praised, she lives!"

Yes, she lives; but the miseries and terrors of the past have shattered the health of Clemence Effingham. Borne by her husband back to the cottage, for weeks she remains helpless, unconscious, hovering on the brink of eternity—while the lesson of penitence, submission, humility, is branded as by fire on the heart of her lord. It is now that the world appears to Effingham, even as it may appear to us all in the light of the last great day: —its treasures, dross; its distinctions, bubbles; its pleasures, a vanishing dream. Now, by the side of his suffering wife, Effingham prays as he prayed when a boy over the grave of a cherished parent; he bows at the foot of the Cross, even as the publican bent in the Temple, feeling himself unworthy so much as to lift up his eyes unto heaven. Dare he ask that a wife so precious may be spared,—that his guardian angel may delay her upward flight, to linger yet in a vale of tears, that she may trace with him, through that dark vale, the strait path to a promised heaven? The heart of the once proud Effingham is broken and contrite now; like the lost coin in the parable, that which was once hidden in the defiling dust of earth is raised again to the light, and the image and superscription of a heavenly King is found to be stamped upon it still.

When Clemence awoke from her state of lethargic unconsciousness, the soft breath of spring came wooingly through the casement, sweet with the perfume of violets, and musical with the song of birds. Young Vincent, pale from recent illness, sat at the foot of her bed, watching, with a face radiant with delight, the first sign of recognition. And whose was the countenance that bent over her with joy more still, but even more intense? whose hand so tenderly clasped hers? whose voice breathed her name in tones of the deepest love? That was a moment whose exquisite bliss repaid the anguish of the past. The darkness of night had indeed rolled away,—the dreary winter was ended; Clemence was beginning, even upon earth, to reap the harvest of light and gladness sown for the upright in heart, who have not chosen their portion here.

CHAPTER XXVI.

A CONTRAST.

EVEN years have flowed on their silent course since the events recorded in the last chapter took place, and we will again glance at Clemence Effingham in the same humble abode. Its aspect, however, is so greatly altered, that at first we shall scarcely recognize it. Its size has been enlarged, though not considerably, and the rich blossoming creepers have mantled it even to the roof, reversing the image of the poet, by "making the *red* one *green*," and rendering the dwelling an object of beauty to the eye of every passing traveller. The little garden is one bed of flowers, radiant with the fairest productions of the spring. If we enter the fairy abode, we find ourselves in a sitting-room which, though small, is the picture of neatness and comfort. A refined taste is everywhere apparent; and there are so many little elegant tokens of affection—framed pictures, worked cushions, and vases filled with bright and beautiful flowers—that we could rather fancy that one of earth's great ones, weary of state, had chosen this for a rural retreat, than that stern misfortune had driven hither a bankrupt and his ruined family.

Clemence, looking scarcely older than when she left her first, splendid abode—for peace and joy seem sometimes to have power to arrest the changing touch of Time—is seated at the open door. Perhaps she sits there to enjoy the soft evening breeze which so gently plays amongst her silky tresses, or she is watching for the return of her husband and Vincent from their daily visit to M——. Effingham, through the exertions of Mr. Gray, has procured a small office in the town—one which, some years ago, he would have rejected with contempt, but the duties of which he now steadily performs, thankful to be able, by honest effort, to earn an independence, however humble. Vincent still pursues his studies at the academy, paying his own expenses by private tuition, and is regarded as the most gifted scholar that M—— has ever been able to boast of.

Clemence is not alone—a lovely little golden-haired girl is beside her, helping, or seeming to help her mother to fasten white satin bows upon a delicate piece of work, so light and fragile in fabric that it might have appeared woven by fairies. It is a wedding gift for Louisa, and will be dearly valued by the bride.

"And, mamma dear," said the child, looking up into the smiling face of Clemence, "is there not something that I could send to sister too?"

"The wild-flowers which you gathered this morning, my darling, in the meadow."

"Oh, but won't they all die on the way?"

"We will press them in a book first, to dry them, and then they will look lovely for years."

"Poor flowers—all crushed down!" sighed little Grace.

"Only preserved," said Clemence; and her words carried a deeper meaning to herself than that which reached the mind of the child.

"I wish I were rich—very rich!" cried little Grace, after a silent pause.

"And what would my May-blossom do with her riches?"

"I would send a cake—such a cake—to sister!" replied Grace, opening her little arms wide to give an idea of its size; "and it should be sugared all over!"

"Anything else?" inquired Clemence.

"I'd make dear Vincy happy—quite happy. He wants so much to go to college and be a clergyman, like Mr. Gray, and teach all the people to be good; but he says that he has not the money. Mamma, don't you wish you had plenty of money?"

"No, my love," replied Clemence, more gravely, parting the golden locks on the brow of her little daughter.

"Martha told me," said Grace, with the air of one in possession of an important secret—"Martha told me that once you had a grand house, and a carriage, and horses, and servants, and dresses—oh, such fine dresses to wear!"

"Long, long ago," replied Clemence.

"Was it when you lived with your dear old uncle, who gave you the pretty little locket which always hangs round your neck?"

"No; I lived very happily with him in a cottage not much larger than this."

Little Grace remained for some moments twirling the white ribbon round her tiny fingers, with a look of thought on her innocent face; then she said reverently,—

"Mamma, did God take away your money?"

"Yes, dearest; in wisdom and love."

"But if you asked Him—if you prayed very hard—would He not give it all back to you again?"

"I should not dare to pray for it, my Grace: I

should not dare even to *wish* for it again. I have been given blessings so much dearer, so much sweeter "—and she stooped to press a kiss on the soft, fair brow of her child. "God has taught me that what makes His people happy is not wealth, but religion and peace and love. I have had more real joy in this little cottage than I ever knew in my large and beautiful home. But, see! there are your father and brother! Quick, quick—run forward to meet them, or the first kiss will not be yours !"

We turn from the sunshine of Willow Cottage to the shady side of the narrow street in which Lady Selina and her nieces for years have made their abode. How have those years sped with the woman of the world?

They have sped in the constant pursuit of pleasure, grasping at shadows, seeking satisfying joys where such are never to be found ; in straining to "keep up appearances," efforts to dress as well, entertain as well as those whose fortunes greatly exceeded her own ; in paying by the self-denial of a month for the ostentatious display of a night; in exchanging rounds of formal visits with acquaintance who would not shed a tear, or forego an hour's mirth, were she to-morrow laid in her grave. Lady

Selina feels her strength decaying, but by artificial
aids she attempts to hide the change from others—
by wilful delusion from herself. She would ignore
sickness, ignore trial, ignore death! And yet, in
hours of solitude and weakness, truth, however unwelcome, will sometimes force its way; and those
whose *all* is contained within the hour-glass of Time
are constrained to watch the sands ever flowing, to
see below the accumulating heap of infirmities,
troubles, and cares, and mark above the hollow, in-
verted cone of ever-lessening pleasures. How miserable, then, is the reflection, that no mortal hand can
restore a single grain, and that, when the last runs
out, nothing will remain but the grave, and the
dark, awful future beyond it.

But Lady Selina spares no effort to banish such
reflections. It is but recently that she has even
mustered courage sufficient for the performance of
the necessary duty of making her will, leaving her
small property to her nephew, Vincent ; perhaps as
a salve to her conscience for utterly neglecting him
during her lifetime. Lady Selina is less willing
than she ever was before to fix her meditations on
death or the grave. She will struggle on to the
last, laden with the vanity which distracts, the prejudice which distorts, the malice which corrodes the
mind. Her temper has become very irritable, for

which her infirmities may offer some excuse; but her peevish nervousness serves to imbitter the lives of the two sisters who have chosen her dwelling as their own.

The haughty Arabella has suffered not less acutely, though more silently than her aunt, from the change in their outward circumstances; but she wraps herself up in selfishness and pride, and though she often finds her present life painful and mortifying, deems it more tolerable than one spent in a cottage, with Clemence Effingham for a companion.

The case is somewhat different with her sister. There have been times when, wearied with a round of amusements, longing for gentle sympathy and affection, wounded by the peevishness of her aunt, or the selfish indifference of Arabella, Louisa has felt almost disposed to accept reiterated invitations to Willow Cottage, and has half resolved to cast in her lot with those nearest and dearest to her heart. But she is like some fluttering insect, caught in the double web of her own habitual love of pleasure and the influence of worldly relatives. Lady Selina ever represents Cornwall as an English Siberia, a desolate wild, in which existence would be perfect stagnation. She paints the gloom which must surround the dwelling of a ruined, disappointed man, till Louisa actually regards her indulgent father with feelings approaching to fear. Arabella is indignant if her sister even alludes to the subject of any change in her arrangements; so, enchained by indolence, folly, and fear, Louisa quietly resigns herself to a position which is often painful as well as unnatural. Her father's kindness permits her a choice; her choice is to remain where pleasure may be found. Her longing for happiness is unsatisfied still, but it is at the world's broken cisterns that she seeks to quench the thirst of an immortal soul.

Lady Selina's ambition is now concentrating itself on one object. Her nieces must form brilliant alliances—they must be united to men of fortune and rank, and in their homes she must find once more the luxury, grandeur, and importance which she once enjoyed in that of their father. The wish so long indulged, and scarcely concealed, appears now to be on the point of partial fulfilment. Sir Mordaunt Strange has offered his hand to Louisa; it has been, after some hesitation, accepted, and every letter to the cottage from Lady Selina is full of encomiums on the character, manner, and appearance of the "Intended," and of felicitations on the happy prospects opening before the young bride elect.

Mr. Effingham and his son are to be present at the wedding. Clemence would fain accompany them to London, for her heart yearns over Louisa, and the very praise so lavishly bestowed upon Sir Mordaunt by Lady Selina excites misgivings in the step-mother's breast. Prudential motives and other obstacles, however, prevent Clemence from accomplishing her wish.

We shall glance for a moment at Louisa, as she stands before a pier-glass in the drawing-room of her aunt, trying on her bridal veil and wreath of white orange-blossoms. A milliner is adjusting the spray which is to fall on the fair girl's graceful neck.

"Stay for a moment," says Lady Selina, walking towards the bride with a feeble step (for she is infirm, though she will not own it, and was more fit for her couch last night than for the gay assembly at which she appeared); "Sir Mordaunt's beautiful diamond spray will make the *coiffure* complete," and she draws from its case a sparkling ornament, which she places upon the brow of her niece. "Look, Arabella, could anything be more charming? The dear child is *mise à peindre!*"

Louisa glances into the mirror with a smile and a blush. It is chiefly by working upon her vanity that her aunt has obtained such influence over her weak and ill-regulated mind. It is an hour of pride to the maiden. About to change her name for a title—her present small abode for a luxurious house of her own—receiving congratulations from every

quarter—her table covered with splendid gifts—
rich jewels glittering on her fair brow—her childish
heart is elated, and for the instant she believes herself happy.   But why, while the blush heightens on
her cheek, has the smile entirely disappeared ?   Why
is the feeling of momentary elation succeeded by
misgiving and gloom ?   The door has opened, and
the bride elect sees reflected in the mirror beside her
own image that of another.   She sees a face, not
plain, but unpleasing—not coarse in its outlines, but
hard in its expression ; she sees him whom she is
about to pledge herself to love, honour, and obey
yet whom she regards with indifference—happy if
indifference be not one day exchanged for fear, mistrust, and aversion !   Louisa Effingham has for the
second time made the world her deliberate choice.
House, carriage, title, jewels, estate,— for such
baubles as these will she, a few days hence, in the
presence of God and man, bind herself to one whom
she loves not, whom she never can learn to love!
Slave to a proud and capricious tyrant, her home
will be but a luxurious prison, and the unhappy
wife will bitterly rue the day when she sold herself
to a bondage more intolerable than that under which
the poor African groans !

    This is the crowning sacrifice to which the world
dooms its willing slaves.   The poor victim goes

crowned to the altar; friends smile, relations congratulate, and admiring spectators applaud. Who would then whisper of a galling yoke, a wounded spirit, a breaking heart; who would whisper that the gold circlet on the finger may be but the first link in a heavy chain? Moloch's shrieking victims were soon destroyed in the flames;—more wretched the fate of those whose slow-consuming pangs make life itself one long sacrifice of woe!

CHAPTER XXVII.

ADY SELINA had succeeded in making "a most eligible marriage" for one of her nieces, but she speedily discovered that she had by no means effected her chief object, that of securing a home for herself. "I am married to Louisa, and not to her family," said Sir Mordaunt, not long after the wedding, and his conduct to his wife's relations accorded with the spirit of his words.

Lady Selina was bitterly disappointed and deeply wounded. The failure of her most cherished project preyed on her spirits, and probably shortened her life. The base ingratitude of mankind, the emptiness of all earthly hopes, became the constant topic of her conversation. But though she could rail against the world in her hours of depression, it was still her most cherished idol. Dagon might be broken, its fair proportion and beauty all destroyed, but the mutilated stump was enthroned on its pedestal of pride, to be honoured and worshipped still !

"Arabella, my dear," said Lady Selina, as one morning she appeared in the breakfast-room at a late hour, wrapped in her dressing-gown, and shivering as if with cold—"Arabella, my dear, I feel so ill, that I wish that you would write and ask the doctor to call."

Arabella was seated at her desk. She had not risen on the entrance of her aunt, nor did she think it in the least necessary to bear her company at her lonely meal. Lady Selina, with a shaking hand, helped herself to some tea, but left the cup unemptied, its contents were so bitter and cold.

"I suppose," said Arabella carelessly, without looking up from her writing, "that you'll not go to the countess's to-night ?"

"I fear I am not equal to the effort, though I was very anxious to be there."

"Then, when the note goes to the doctor, William can take one at the same time to Lady Praed, to ask her to chaperon me to the concert."

"If you wish it," replied the lady faintly. "Would you be so good, my dear, as to close that window ? the cold seems to pierce through my frame."

"Cold! nonsense, aunt! How can you talk of cold on such a grilling morning as this? If I were to keep the window shut we should be stifled, there's not a breath of air in this hot, narrow street."

Lady Selina was too weak and languid to dispute the point with her niece; she only sighed, shivered, and drew her wrapper closer around her.

The day was a long, weary one to Lady Selina; she spent it chiefly in peevish complainings, to which the only listeners were her medical man and her maid. Towards evening, however, she rallied; and Arabella was surprised on descending to the drawing-room, to await the arrival of Lady Praed, to find Lady Selina there, also ready attired for the concert. What mocking brilliancy appeared in the diamonds which gleamed beside those ghastly and withered features! How ill the robe of amber satin beseemed the shrunken form that wore it! The painful incongruity, however, did not attract the attention of Arabella.

"I wish, aunt, that you knew your own mind," she said impatiently to Lady Selina; "if you were determined to go yourself, there was no need to ask a favour of Lady Praed. I really don't see now how we are to manage; we have not ordered our own carriage, and there will not be room in hers for three. My new dress will be crushed to a mummy!" and the young lady shook out the rustling folds with a very dissatisfied air.

Whether in consideration to Arabella's *moire antique*, or (as is more probable) from feeling herself, when the moment for decision arrived, quite unable to go to the party, Lady Selina, on Lady Praed's calling for her niece, finally determined on remaining behind. Arabella did not conceal her satisfaction, and passed her evening gaily amongst a fashionable throng, without giving even a thought to the poor invalid, except when inquiries concerning her health were made as a necessary form, and answered with careless unconcern.

It was midnight when Arabella returned. The servant, as she entered the house of her aunt, addressed her with the words, "Her ladyship has not yet gone to her room."

"Not gone to rest yet! that's strange!" cried Arabella; and with rather a quickened step she proceeded at once to the room in which she had left Lady Selina.

The candles had burned down to their sockets; the light of one had died out, and only a curling line of dark smoke issued from the fallen wick; the other cast around its dull, yellow light, revealing to the eye of Arabella a scene which even her proud, cold spirit could not contemplate without a sensation of horror.

A form still sat upright in its high-backed, cushioned chair,—a form attired in amber satin, and adorned with magnificent gems ; but the ghastly hue of death was on the brow, the glaze of death on the dull, fixed eye, the hand hung down motionless and stiff. Arabella uttered a faint cry, for the first glance was sufficient to reveal to her the terrible truth—she was gazing on the corpse of Lady Selina !

CHAPTER XXVIII.

NCE again we will pass over seven years— their lights and shades, their joys and their sorrows—and join on their path over the fresh green-sward, bright with dew-drops that glitter in the sunshine, a party on their way to an ivy-mantled church. We recognize at a glance the tall, manly form of Effingham, though there are now deeper lines on his features, and broader streaks of silver in his hair. Perhaps we may also trace in his countenance an expression of thought more subdued and earnest,—the expression of one who has known much of the trials of life, but who has had the strength to rise above them,—an expression brightening into cheerfulness whenever his gaze is bent on the gentle partner who rests on his arm.

The face of Clemence can never lose its charm, for it wears *the beauty of holiness,*—that beauty which time has no power to wither, and eternity it-self can but perfect. Grace is at her mother's side, a bright and blooming girl, whose type may be found in the fragrant blush-rose which she has culled in passing from the spray.

But whose is the drooping form, clad in widow's attire, which Mr. Effingham supports with the gentle tenderness of compassion? It is a bruised reed, a withered blossom,—one over which the harrow has passed—one which the rude foot has trodden down. Louisa, broken-spirited and weary of the world, has come to seek rest in her father's home, as a wander-ing bird, pierced by the shaft of the fowler, with quivering wing and ruffled down flies back to the shelter of its nest.

" Mother !" exclaimed Grace, " you once told me that you had but one great earthly wish unfulfilled, and that was to see our dear Vincent in the pulpit, preaching the gospel of peace. That last wish will be gratified to-day, mother ; are you now quite happy ? "

" As happy, I believe, as a mortal can be on this side heaven," replied Clemence ; and the beaming sunshine in her blue eyes, as she raised them for a moment towards the calm sky, expressed more even than her words.

" That Vincent should ever have devoted himself

to the ministry, giving his whole heart to its duties, is mainly owing, I believe," said Mr. Effingham, " to the influence of your mother."

"Oh ! Vincent always says," exclaimed Grace, " that he was the most wayward and wilful of boys, and that any good that he may ever do in this world is owing to her prayers and example."

Effingham bent down his head, so that his voice should reach the ear of his wife alone,—" Vincent's father has yet more cause," he murmured, " to bless those prayers and that example."

Clemence entered the church with a heart so full of gratitude, peace, and love, that there seemed left in it no room for a worldly care or an earthly regret. Through infirmity, weakness, and sorrow, she had humbly endeavoured to follow her Lord, and He had led her from darkness to light,—He had turned even her trials into blessings. Had she resigned wealth in obedience to His will ? He had made poverty itself the channel by which the riches of His grace had been freely poured into her bosom. In poverty her husband's affection had deepened,— that affection which, for the sake of conscience, she had hazarded to weaken or to lose ; in poverty her son, removed from evil influence, had learned lessons of self-denial, faith, and love, which would make him her *joy and crown* through the ages of a blissful eternity; in poverty her own character had been strengthened,—she had learned more fully, more submissively to trust the love of her heavenly Father : and now her cup overflowed with blessings, —blessings which she need not fear freely to enjoy ; for it was the smile of her Lord that had changed the waters of bitterness to the wine of gladness; it was from His hand that she had received her treasures—and those treasures were *not* her idols.

> Whatever comes between the soul and Christ, the Fount of Light
>   Must cast a shadow on the soul, how fair soe'er it seem.
> Yet need we not resign earth's choicest blessings,—all is bright
>   When what we love *obstructs not* but *reflects* the heavenly beam